BITTER

FAMILY SECRETS

Book #3

This book ties it
all together !

♡ Vick Brudy
2017

BITTER

FAMILY SECRETS

VICK BREEDY

Acknowledgements:

Thank you, God, for giving me the motivation and discipline to write Bitter Family Secrets. I am thankful for the unconditional support of my family. There's nothing like family. Thank you, Team Bitter, for keeping the Bitter Movement going. There would be no movement if you didn't support my vision. This I know. Thank you to all of the people that have read Bitter and Still Bitter. Thank you for telling a friend to tell a friend about my books. Thank YOU for reading this book.

Dedication:

I dedicate this book to all of the women that took a negative situation and flipped it into a positive one. I dedicate this book to all of the men that took the high road when it was easier to be petty. I dedicate this book to the men and women that chose to forgive when "they" never said sorry. I dedicate this book to the women that made it through the storm and came out stronger on the other side. I dedicate this book to the men that decided to take the uncomfortable route, in order to grow. I dedicate this book to the men and women that've had their hearts crushed, but are still able to love. I dedicate this book to the women that decided to let God handle him, instead of throwing a brick through his window shield. If this is you; I dedicate this book to you.

Edited by Elijah Jean Editing.

Table of Contents:

Where Things Left Off

Karma:

Still Bitter Private Investigating Agency is no more. I had to shut that shit down. With my mom dead and my sister Eve living back in Charlotte, I had no motivation or desire to keep the agency open. Lance bought the agency off me and changed the name to Closet Investigations. His agency caters to the LGBTQ community.

To this day, Lance still thinks of himself as my uncle. He truly is my mom's best friend. He's treated me like I was his flesh and blood throughout my entire existence. When my mother was murdered, he stepped in and stepped up. He made all her funeral arrangements. He also made sure that I was eating and washing myself. It sounds basic, but when you experience a traumatic loss, self-care doesn't feel important. Lance made it a point to tell me that he'd be checking in on me regularly. On the surface, it sounded like a compassionate gesture, but it was a warning. He knows me. He knows how I get down. He knows of my addiction. My grandmother was too distraught to take the lead - at least, that's how she acted. It feels like forever, but it's been a month. The police still have no leads on my mother's homicide. I wonder if they are even investigating it. After all, she was Craig's cousin.

As I was going through my stages of grief, my grandmother was all up in my mix. She irritated the hell out of me. I ended up having to kick her ass out of our house. My mom left everything to me. She had more money than I thought. I was able to buy my grandmother a newly constructed ranch style home in Milton, MA. I also bought her a car. Her old behind had the nerve to want a Land Rover. Since I had the money, I got it for her. I also put half a million dollars in her bank account. I figured that ought to keep her out of my hair for a while. I was right. I haven't seen or heard from my grandmother in weeks. My mother always said that my grandmother wasn't shit. I thought she would have at least come back to get her jewelry that she asked me to hold.

During my time of grief, I'll admit, I was acting like a whore. I even slept with Eve's ex man, Richard. That shit was off the chain. He was visiting his family for something--I forget what for. After my mother's funeral, I ran into him at Slade's. We talked. I asked him about his brother and how he was doing. He knew that we dated for a while. I told him the story about how we broke up. The more we talked, the more honest I started feeling. Before I knew it, I'd admitted that I cheated on his brother because he couldn't keep up with my sexual appetite.

To my surprise, he didn't defend his brother. Instead, he told me that his sexual appetite may be just as strong as mine. My coochie started encouraging me to see what Richard was working with. I'd heard some stories about how Richard put it down in the bedroom from Eve so I wanted to confirm it. After a few drinks, we ended up back at my house. To my surprise, he could hang with me. We fucked for three hours and only stopped for water breaks. I may have met my match.

Eve doesn't know that I fucked her ex-boyfriend. She also doesn't know that I know she killed Cynthia. I could tell even through her disguise that it was Eve. I pay attention to people, especially their body language. The surveillance video only allowed viewers to see Eve from behind. Someone else might not recognize her, but I sure did. She had a specific stride about her. I never told Uncle Craig. I know that he'd kill Eve if he found out she killed his fiancé. I decided to keep this piece of information to myself. I haven't seen Richard since then. He's back in Charlotte. Eve went back to Charlotte to talk to her mother. I wonder if she is going to try to hook up with Richard again. Now, I know first-hand why she said she was dickmatized. His dick

8

is worth me taking a plane ride to Charlotte to get some more. But I'll be good. After all, Eve is my sister.

BJ:

After I saw Karma fucking her sister's ex-boyfriend, I knew she was dangerous. There's no way that she could have a functioning conscience and fuck Richard. She has an evil side to her. Since the day I walked in on her and Richard doing the nasty, I've stayed away from her. Richard didn't see me, but she did. This crazy bitch had big balls. Karma actually motioned for me to join them as Richard was delivering his dick to her. She's really sick.

Just because I participated in a threesome with her once, doesn't mean that I'll do it again. I didn't really even agree to it the first time. She tricked me. She got me all hot and bothered and then invited dick - without my permission - into my pussy. I allowed it to happen, because I wanted to please her. I let some guy I never met before fuck me from behind while I ate Karma's cookie. The dumb stuff we do for love.

For some reason, she won't pick sides. She's goes back and forth between pussy and dick. At first, I thought she was a lesbian that wouldn't admit to preferring pussy over dick. I've learned that I'm wrong. Karma is obsessed with dick and every once in a while, will entertain pussy, just to keep it interesting. She's a freak. Not a lesbian.

Out of the blue, Karma texts me. She says that she has a business plan that she wants to discuss with me and wants to know if I want to go into business with her. I can't imagine what type of business she wants to start. Interested in finding out, I agree to meet with her. I make sure

9

to request we meet in a public location. With a lot of people around, she won't be able to put her sexual sorcery on me with.

Again, I am wrong. Karma is dressed in a fire engine red wrap dress and nude open-toe high heels. As she walks towards me, her dress opens to her upper thigh with each stride. She is looking good. Her hair is down. It is parted down the middle and bone straight. She definitely has a weave. Her hair rests at the top of her hard nipples. She isn't wearing a bra.

I'm expecting her to say "Hello" and give me a hug. But I know that would be too normal for Karma. Instead, she walks right up to me and grabs my pussy with her hand. She leaves it there while she French kisses me. I'm shocked, instantly turned on and embarrassed. My face turns red and my bud swells up. I told you this bitch is dangerous. I have a hard time concentrating as she decides to get right down to business. She acts like she didn't just sexually assault me in public – as if what she did was as normal as a hand shake. She's not phased. She already knows she won. I already know it too. I'm going to do whatever it is that she wants me to.

Eve:

When I arrive in Charlotte, I have a hard time finding Gina. The bitch moved. I wasn't expecting that. It caught me off guard so I ask around to find out where she disappeared to. Word on the street is that she moved to South Carolina with some addict that she met at an NA meeting. While she was out there, she started using again. Gina was in South Carolina for only a month. When she returned to Charlotte, she was in worse condition than when she left. I heard she's now strung out and lives at one of those motels where they let you pay week to week. I also heard that these days, she's sucking dick to get money. I guess old habits are hard to break. Better her than me. I'll find out which one of those motels she's staying at soon enough.

Since I'm back in Charlotte and can't find Gina, I take a chance at reaching out to my ex-boyfriend Richard. I must have picked the wrong week, because nobody seems to be in Charlotte. When I call, he tells me that he is in Massachusetts. I was hoping to talk to him face-to-face. I know that we weren't on the best terms with each other, but he is blatantly blowing me off. He is either busy or could care less about talking to me. I can't determine which one it is. I will admit that I am disappointed in his reaction to my call. I was hoping he'd be here and be happy to see me. Nope. He blew me off. When he is hanging up the call, I hear a bitch's voice in the background. Instantly, I get an attitude. This man's outright rejection has me so messed up that I start hearing things. The voice sounds like it is Karma's. There's no way he'd be in the company of Karma. I'm tripping.

I call my cousin Casey to see if I can stay with her for a while. I'm not sure how long I am going to be in Charlotte so I need a place to lay my head while I figured things out. The sit-down conversation I intended to have with Gina may not happen how I want it to. With her being in the condition that she's in, I'd get nowhere. Shit never goes according to plan. One would think that I'd have enough sense to come out here with a Plan B. Nope. Now, it's looking like I'll need a Plan C too.

I'm not sure if I will be returning to Massachusetts or moving to a new state. Still Bitter Private Investigating Agency died right along with Ava. Karma gave everyone a generous severance package. I will be straight for a little while. I will eventually need a job wherever I decide to go. Initially, I only planned on staying down here a few days before heading back to

11

Boston. However, after receiving that text message, I kind of got spooked. It may be a little too hot for me in Boston to return any time soon.

They only sent the message once, but once was enough to rattle me. I was very careful when I went into the hospital to kill Cynthia. The nurse that let me in, saw the disguised me. She didn't have my contact info. Even if she tried to reach me, she'd have gotten the wrong number because I used a fake number on the sign in sheet. Someone is definitely trying to fuck with me. I need to find out who it is. They'll reveal themselves soon enough. When they do, I'll see what it is that they want from me. Then, I'll take it from there.

Casey's place smells like weed. I can tell she tried to air it out because she knew that I was coming through. Unfortunately, she failed at that attempt. I got contact high just walking through her door. She had some Rick Ross song playing in the background. The décor is black and red. She has an oversized black faux leather sectional. Above it is a huge ceiling fan. I'm guessing that it doesn't work because she doesn't have it on. So much for not smelling like a joint.

***

Richard has been on my mind a lot lately. I woke up his morning feeling cranky. I almost forgot that I had a dream about him last night until something reminded me of him. While I was watching TV a commercial came on that bragged about their product being so good that customers won't want to put it down. I used to refer to Richard as "Mr. Put it Down and Shut It Down". I really miss the sex that we used to have. He'd do it to me so well; then he'd tear it up so I couldn't get any from someone else.

The dream that I had wasn't a good one. I dreamt that I found out that he was diagnosed with HIV. I remember feeling fear in my dream. I was afraid that I may have been exposed to it too. My feelings for him went from lust to hate.

My entire life passed before my eyes in my dream. In a matter of seconds, I went through all the stages of grief. I am so THANKFUL that it was only a dream. I thought about how that could have easily been a reality because we had more unprotected sex than protected sex. I thought about the dream again and felt a feeling of relief. It was just a dream. Maybe, that was God's way of telling me to slow my roll. To think that I came here ready to meet up with Richard and hopefully get some dick in the process. I don't know who he's been doing since we been apart. I don't know if he used condoms with them. I don't know much of anything. That dream may have saved my life. I'll most definitely pass on the dick if he offers it.

I get up off Casey's living room sofa and head to the bathroom to pee. Immediately, I'm disgusted. This cousin of mine got a period puddle on the toilet seat. How could she not see that she left that there before she walked out? One thing Gina did teach me is to make sure I don't leave any bodily fluids around after using the bathroom. She taught me to always do a once over to make sure I didn't leave anything nasty or embarrassing behind for the next person.

So, before I can pee, I have to wipe up after Casey like she's my pre-teen that doesn't know any better. Even after I disinfect the toilet I decide to squat my pee out instead of sitting comfortably on the seat. The visual is still too fresh for me to sit down on the toilet. Once I'm done relieving myself, I wash my hands and brush my teeth. When I'm done, I realize there's no towel in the bathroom to dry my hands. It makes me wonder if this nasty ass cousin of mine ever washes her hands.

13

The more I look around, the more turned off I'm getting. I need to make sure that my bags are zipped. I see small black turds that look like ice cream jimmies in the corner where the tooth brush cup is kept. I pull back the shower curtain and I see a roach chilling right at the rim of the drain. The tub has a ring around it and there are, what look like pubic hairs, sprinkled on the base of the tub. I'm not taking a shower here. I'm not staying here another moment. What is up with dirty ass bitches these days! I shake my shit out before I repack my bag and leave Casey's without showering. For the next few days I'm going to stay at a hotel until I figure out my next move.

I leave Casey a note thanking her for letting me crash at her place. I tell her that I'll holla at her in a few. I'm not sure when I'll be back over here or if I will be back over here for that matter. I don't know what happened to Casey but I know her mom is a neat freak. When Casey lived with her mom, I would sometimes spend the night over. There were no roaches or mice. Casey's dirty ass should be ashamed. Her mom definitely taught her better than this. I'm the one that had the crack head for a parent. Wow! It just registered. If Gina is not my mother, then Casey is not my cousin.

Claudia:

I know that the cleaning girl has been stealing from me. Just wait until she comes here next week. I'm going to cuss her thieving behind out. Can't trust nobody these days! I pay the Spanish bitch to clean my house, not clean me out. She's fired. I'm not going to fire her until I see her though. I want to cuss her out face-to-face.

I can't find any of my diamond jewelry. My diamond tennis bracelet is gone. My diamond cocktail rings are gone. My diamond hoop earrings are gone. I bet she would have taken my diamond studs too if I didn't have them in my ear. After further investigation, I learned that all my gold jewelry is gone too. I can't stand people that steal.

There's just something about stealing that disturbs me. If you are low on cash, ask to borrow some money. Don't take it upon yourself to decide for someone that they'll be ok without their possessions. What type of shit is that? I hope that the guilt keeps the bitch up at night. Some of that stuff I can never get back. Some of it was custom made. There were old pieces from my childhood stolen from me. The more that I think about it, the angrier I get.

To keep myself from getting too worked up. I decide to take a drive. My plans are to drive down 93 and pop in on my granddaughter Karma. It's been a while since I've seen her. I know this sounds crazy, but for the life of me, I can't remember how to get to the house. This is the fifth time I've tried to take this drive and end up lost. I don't even have the address written down. I could call her, but she'd think I was fucking with her if I asked her for the address.

I think I need to see a doctor. My memory is getting worse each week. I'm in my early seventies. I shouldn't be forgetting like this. If it gets worse, I will make an appointment with my primary care physician. Hopefully, I'm just tripping. I can't see myself in no old folks' home because I keep forgetting shit. I've always been very independent. I don't have any kids to take care of me. The one kid that I have acts like she doesn't know me. That's why I want to head to the house to visit Karma. I need to find out where Ava moved to.

Karma:

Well ain't this some shit! A bitch is pregnant. I figured that my period was just late. However, my instincts told me that I better buy myself a pregnancy test to see what's up. This was not a part of the plan. I know whose baby it is--that's what makes this such a big NO, NO. I can't have my sister's ex-boyfriend's baby. That would be so scandalous. My mom had a baby with her ex-husband's brother. That's how I got here. I'm not about to follow those footsteps.

My mom was a hot mess. When she was still alive, she told me that she enjoyed knowing that her ex-husband Brian was my uncle. I can't help but laugh. She really stuck it to him. She told me the story about how Uncle Brian cheated on her. So, to get revenge she cheated on him with his brother. It wasn't actually cheating. They were divorced when it happened. Regardless, she was still wrong for doing him. Ava told me that it wasn't her intention to have a baby by my dad Ben. Once she found out that she was pregnant, there was no turning back. She wouldn't abort me.

I am not my mother. This baby is as good as gone. I'm a pro-choice individual. Plus, I am too young to be having a baby. I have a whole lot of living to do before I can imagine a kid in the picture. Besides, my figure is too fit to be messing it up with a baby. Now is not the time for all that. I do want to have a child one day, but not today. And I don't want to repeat my mother's fuck-up. I'd be having a baby with my ex-boyfriend's brother. Sorry mom. I know you'd want me to look at it as a blessing, but right now it just feels like a sick joke.

I call my gynecologist and schedule an appointment to have a pregnancy test at her office. They have a cancellation so they can get me in at 4:30pm today.

"Hi Karma."

"Hi Dr. Fielding."

"What brings you in today?"

"Didn't your assistant write down why I'm in here today?" I say with an attitude.

"Why don't you tell me why you are here so that we can move forward?"

"Look I'm sure that you are just doing your job, but you and I both know why I am here. I'm confirming what I already know. I'm pregnant and I want an abortion. There's no need in telling me my options. I already know them. I just need this to happen as quickly as possible so I can move on with my life. "

"Karma, I show you nothing but respect whenever you are in my office. I expect that you do the same. You know that I was friends with your mother. . ."

"You two couldn't have been too friendly. I didn't see you at the funeral" I snap.

"You know something Karma, I'm not even going to go there with you. I will have my nurse set you up with an appointment with my colleague Dr. Manning. He can see you the soonest. I don't want to live with the fact that you are killing your mother's first grandchild. Ava might come back from the dead to teach me a lesson. You and I both know that Ava didn't play. She believed in revenge like it was a religious practice." She says this and walks out the room.

Eve:

Richard is being such a bitch. We've talked on the phone a few times since I've been here, but he refuses to meet up with me face to face. At first, I thought that it was because he couldn't trust himself around me. That's clearly not the case.

Last night, I decided to see just what he was up to. I parked my rental car in front of his house then made myself comfortable and sat in the back seat. The windows in the back of this Prius are tinted. I didn't know how long I'd have to wait for him to come home, but I was prepared to stay all night.

While I was at the hotel, I made sure I emptied my bladder. I didn't bring anything to drink with me. I didn't bring anything to drink with me because I didn't want to be tempted with the need to go to the bathroom. I couldn't risk missing Richard. I have a key to his place. I know he didn't change the locks. I could wait in his bedroom for him but I decide not to. Hopefully, that is where we end up tonight.

Halfway into my Halloween size bag of Tootsie Rolls, Richard pulls up. My heart flutters when I see him. I'm happy to see him. He looks delicious. The only thing that he has on him that doesn't look good is some tall dark skin chick. *Who the fuck is this bitch? Why is she going into his place? Did I just see this motherfucker smack her on the ass as she walked up the steps?*

I look way better than her. He has definitely lowered his standards by messing around with this average looking chick. I do a quick assessment while I can. Shoes--Payless. Outfit--Target. Her weave is old and is in need of a redo. Her hair looks like it stinks. That's all I could

18

assess in the short amount of time that I saw her. She's whack! And so is he for hooking up with her.

Jealousy swoops in on me and attacks. I'm clearly not over Richard. I can't stand to see him interested in someone else. It's definitely fucking with me. I was hoping to work things out with him and pick right back up where we left off. I see that's not happening. If I can't have love, I will settle for revenge. He made me love him and then just threw me away when things became a little tough. I can't wait for the both of them to leave. I got something for those two.

All night, I stay in the car. I end up having to urinate in a plastic red Dollar Store cup. I poured the pee outside onto the street. I must have gotten a little on the car floor because I could smell a faint odor of pee. Good thing this isn't my car. If it wasn't a rental, I'd be heated! Since this ain't my shit *"oh well."*

I dozed off for a little bit and awoke in the middle of the night. My instincts told me that if his hoe doesn't leave by 2AM, she is spending the entire night. I set my alarm clock on my cell phone for 5AM. I sleep until then. An hour later, Richard is at the door tongue kissing his new boo goodbye. For a moment, I was having second thoughts about getting back at him. But after seeing him slobber all over her, those second thoughts disappeared.

After my replacement left, Richard leaves thirty minutes later. Unless something has changed, he will be gone to work for at least nine hours. That leaves me with plenty of time to go to Home Depot to get the supplies that I need. When I get to Home Depot, the smell of wood suffocates me as I walk through the home improvement store's door. I walk toward the aisle that houses the cement.

Richard seems to have no love or longing for me in his heart. He hasn't shown any pain from losing me. He kept it moving and moved on. I plan on moving on too--right after I make sure that he feels my pain. Richard needs to suffer. He has no right to treat me the way he did. He gets mad at me one time and then drops me. I thought that I meant more to him.

I walk out of Home Depot with all the supplies that I need. I'm in straight bitch mode. I left him alone in the beginning because I really thought that we'd get back together at some point. I thought that he'd move up to Boston with me. He didn't. He acts like he never knew me. It's crazy how people can love you one day and then switch it up the next. This leads me to believe that he was fronting all along.

Richard needs to be taught a lesson and I'm going to be the one to teach him that lesson. I get back to his house and let myself in with the key. Nobody is here, but I'm creeping around like there is. My nerves are fucking with me. I need to settle down. To help take the load of, I decide to go relax and chill. I go right to his room and lay down on his bed.

My nerves immediately calm down. As I am laying here, I start to think about all the nasty things Richard and I did in this bed. I feel my mouth involuntarily curve into a smile. I wonder if he still has any of the videos we made. I wouldn't be surprised if he kept them. Curious to find out, I sit up and bend over the side of the bed. He used to keep the videos in the drawers that are set in the platform of the bed.

Bingo! They are here but they aren't the only ones. It seems that he's added some to the collection. I take the few that aren't featuring me and smash them with a hammer. My nerves are acting up again. I put the smashed videos back where I found them and lay back down on the bed. I locate the first nasty video that we made and just stare at it. The label is written in marker in my handwriting. I labeled it "Beat it up" with a happy face drawn on it.

Memories of he and I making love to each other begin coming back to me. As I am inserting our video into his DVD player, I get a good idea. The video is in and I turn the volume all the way up. The sound of our love making is a big turn on. I'm walking back to the bed we used to share. There are two pillows on the bed, but he only uses the one on the left. My pants and panties are now off and I'm touching myself while on top of his pillow. My moist pussy is planted directly on his pillow case. I'm grinding the pillow as I watch us make love on the TV screen.

I watch Richard take me from behind. He is thrusting in and out with so much force, but I'm taking it. He's talking all types of shit to me and I'm loving it. Just when he's about to climax in the video, I have an intense orgasm and let my juices leak all over his pillow case. I came in the video at the same time I came on his pillow case. Once I recover, I straighten out his bed. I wipe my coochie with the pillow on the right side just in case some bitch sleeps over. They will both get a whiff of my coochie.

Thinking about another bitch got me mad again. I'm not trying to be up in his place all night. If I am going to make him pay for hurting and abandoning me, I have to get started. Play time is over. I go to each bathroom and pour the cement that I bought from the store into his toilet. I then pour it into his tub and sink. If he has a little bit of sense, he will be changing his locks after finding his bathroom fucked up.

With that in mind, I unplug his refrigerator and leave the doors open. I hope he's hungry when he comes home. By then the food will have spoiled. After that, I go into his cabinets and take out all the boxed goods and canned goods. I take a few boxes of Kraft Macaroni and Cheese for me to eat at the hotel. By the time, I'm done in the kitchen, all his boxed goods are opened and emptied onto the floor. Although it was very tedious, I used the can opener to open every canned good in his kitchen. Once opened, I poured them all in his oven. He had all types Goya beans and vegetables in his oven. I hope he doesn't preheat anything without opening the oven first. On second thought I hope he does.

I'm feeling very satisfied. Just as I'm about to leave, my stomach starts hurting me. I feel like I have to take a shit. By this time, the toilets are hard with cement. There's nothing going down his plumbing any time soon. I can't even use the sink like that white girl did in the movie *Bridesmaids* because I poured cement down that drain too. There are two options. I can leave and try to hold it until I get back to the hotel or I can just shit on top of the cement in the toilet.

I pick option two. You know you always have to pee a little before you shit. That's what I do. I pee on top of the cemented toilet bowl and then leave him a nice healthy brown specimen bathing in my urine. I wipe my ass with the toilet paper and throw it on the floor. Fuck him. I leave and lock the door behind me.

BJ:

I've been having that awful nightmare again. It's the one where I'm back in Africa and they are getting ready to perform that barbaric ritual and mutilate my clitoris. I always wake up right before they start cutting me with the same butcher knife they used on the girl before me. My heart rate has sped up tremendously. There's sweat on my nose and on my back. My back is

22

soaked. My Fly Native tee-shirt is sticking to me. I'm cold. I'm afraid. It takes me a while to settle down. It seems so real.

When I was eleven, my mom sent me to live with my aunt and uncle. She explained to me that she wasn't going to be able to stop the elders from hurting me. Having me go and live with her sister was a must. The only way she could save me from that terrifying fate was to ship me off to America. She had to protect me. This was the only way.

I didn't want to leave my mother. I only remember Aunt Clara from pictures. My mom said that my aunt left when I was very young. She met an American man, fell in love and moved to Massachusetts. I was going to live with a relative that I barely knew. I wondered if it was worth it. I'd be escaping torture, but leaving the woman that was my everything. I had no say in the matter.

My mom traveled with me to Massachusetts. I remember the trip feeling like it took forever. She stayed with me at my Aunt Clara's home for a month. Then she left. Before leaving, she said that I couldn't come back home until I was older and hopefully married. I cried. I knew she was going to have hell to pay once she got back home. I cried for my mother every day for two weeks. I was in a foreign land with relatives I just met. Everything was so new and unfamiliar. I was lonely and afraid. I wanted to go back to Africa. Massachusetts was nothing like Ethiopia.

My mom told me that she would come back and see me within a few years, not a few months, like I hoped. That was too much for me to bare. I had no idea how much of a financial hardship the trip caused my mother. I had no idea when I was going to see her again. One day, I overheard her talking to my aunt about leaving me here. My mom felt that her daughter's safety was worth the sacrifice of not being able to see her grow up. It was worth any punishment inflicted by the elders. She too had been a victim of female circumcision. Since then, she vowed to never let her child endure what she had to.

My Grandparents forced my mom to get butchered. They didn't care that it would affect her self-esteem and her sexual experiences throughout her life. My mom told me stories about her suffering with constant vaginal infections. The tribal mutilator destroyed her vagina. She admitted that sex was painful for her. In her tribe, she was taught that sex wasn't for the woman to enjoy--it was only for the man to enjoy.

When my mom had me, she had to be cut open because her vaginal opening was too small to allow for the passage of a baby. The same thing was done to her mother. She said that my grandmother was cut open the first time she was to be intimate with my grandfather. However, unlike my mother, my grandmother had an *actual* physical barrier. Mom described it as a covered seal.

It's called infibulation. I had to look that shit up. I wondered how the seal was formed. After reading, I understood why infibulation is the worst form of female genital mutilation. The seal is formed by cutting and removing part--sometimes all-- of the clitoris. They then cut and reposition the labia minor and labia majora and sew them together to form a "seal" over the vagina. A small hole is left only to pee.   I learned that there are at least 29 countries that have communities that practice FGM. It's hard to believe that this was and still is a cultural norm that continues to happen in parts of Africa.

I can't imagine living like that. Sex is supposed to feel good. My mom described sex as a woman's duty. It is saddening to know that my mom will never know what it feels like to have

24

her clitoris licked until it becomes a swollen bud. She will never know what it feels like to have an orgasm from clitoral stimulation. She's missed out on so much. I will never be able to repay her or thank her enough for shipping me to my aunt. Although, I missed out on having my mom throughout my teenage years, I understand it was necessary.

She made sure that I was given the chance to have healthy relationships and a healthy sense of self. Years later, when I came out to her, she was upset and disgusted. She said that she didn't send me to America so that I can have other females lick on my vagina. My mom was very homophobic. She couldn't help it though. It's what she was taught. Two years after coming out, she finally accepted the fact that I am gay. She said, at the end of the day, she's happy that I have something for someone to lick on and no longer cared if it was a man or a woman. It's strange that so many years later, I am still dreaming about this ritual. It haunts me.

When I came out to my Aunt Clara, she wasn't trying to hear it either. I'd started calling my Aunt Clara "Mom" after a year of living with her. She went back to being "Aunt Clara" the day she cussed me out about being a dyke. To this day, she's not feeling my "nasty little lifestyle." I'm grown now. I no longer live with my aunt and uncle, so it's all good. I visit them on holidays and we deliberately stay away from any conversations that might remind Aunt Clara that I am gay.

I fall back asleep and have another dream. I dreamed that Karma invited me over last night. I told myself that it was going to be trouble if I go over there. It was a self-fulfilled prophecy. A whole lot of licking took place at Karma's last night. She used all her toys on me. She enjoyed fucking me with her dildo. She kept ordering me to tell her that I liked dick. I did as I was told. She'd kiss me and I'd melt. I was just happy to be spending time with Karma. The intimacy was a bonus. I'm in love with Karma. She told me that she loves me too. I wish that it wasn't a dream.

Karma:

Abortions are no joke. It took me out of commission for a few, but I'm back. The doctor told me that I may have feelings of remorse, but that hasn't happened yet. I'm not ready for a baby. I definitely wasn't going to have one by my sister's ex-boyfriend. That baby had no chance. I'm still trying to figure out what I want to do with my life. I'm in no positon to be responsible for another human being. There should be more people like me in the world instead of females having four and five babies, knowing that they can't take care of one. Then those little bastards grow up. They grow up to become big bastards. We wonder why there's so many crazy motherfuckers out there. They're out there because there aren't enough women like me in the world. I had enough sense to end that shit before it became a problem for everyone.

I met with BJ to discuss my business idea. I want to start running groups and seminars to help women and men spice up their relationship. Ava was a good teacher. She groomed me for this. My mother groomed me to be my husband's everything in the bedroom. I'd like to teach couples how to do this. I don't know what type of business this would be or if I would need any type of license or certificate. So, I figured I'd reach out to BJ and see if she knew anything. When we met, she told me that if I took the motivational speaker approach, I wouldn't need any credentials. I looked at her and smiled. Now all I needed was to figure out how I was going to

26

spin this to make it into motivational speaking. What I really want is to motivate people to get the best out of their bedroom experience. I kissed BJ on the lips and then licked them before I left. I told her that I'd hit her up once I had more details figured out.

That girl is sprung. She told me that she would help me in any way that I needed. I knew what that meant. She wanted to spend some bedroom time with me. I will save that card for when I really need her to pull through for me. She may need a motivational fuck. Right now, I need her mind to be right. I've noticed that once she starts dealing with me, she becomes too focused on me and neglects other shit. I can't have her neglecting my shit. So, she won't be getting any from me until it's absolutely necessary.

My doorbell rings. I'm not expecting anyone. My attitude changes. It's either someone I don't want to be bothered with or a delivery. I try to think back to see if I ordered anything online. I did. I ordered a few autobiographies. I head to the door hoping that it's my books. It's not. It's that bitch who has been missing in action - my grandmother.

I wonder why she came by today. I also wonder why she is ringing the bell. Too lazy to use the key that she never gave back. I look her up and down. She looked stressed the hell out. I don't know what she has to be stressed about. She's got access to whatever she wants. She doesn't have to lift a finger. She has a maid that I pay to cook and clean for her. However, since she said that she doesn't trust someone cooking for her, she does her own cooking. That's the only work she does, but she doesn't have to.

When I opened the door, and saw her standing outside, I was about to tell her that she looked a mess. Something about her facial expression stops me from saying that to her. She looks worn out, as if she had a few rough nights. She looks confused. I tell her to come in before she lets a bug fly in.

My grandmother walks into the kitchen without saying hello. I wonder what her problem is. Instinctively, I make some mint tea for the both of us. She sits in silence and so do I. I'm not going to speak until she does. I'm ok with silence. Most people tend to get uncomfortable with silence and feel the need to fill it in with words. I am not one of those people. We both sit at the kitchen island and sip tea. By the time that I am halfway done with my tea she finally says something.

"Where's your mother at these days?"

I don't answer her. I look at her like *What the fuck did she just ask me?*

"You lose your hearing or did you lose your tongue?"

I continue to look at her as if she's lost her mind. I say nothing.

"I don't know what your problem is. You need to show some respect when I'm addressing you. Can you answer the damn question?"

"Where is this going? Why are you asking me some shit like that and what the fuck is your problem?"

That confused look appears on her face again. As soon as it there, it's gone and replaced with a look of disgust.

"You little bitch" she says in a calm manner. She continues to tell me off.

"I don't know why I'd expect you to be a better woman than your trifling ass mother. You came from her, which means you have pieces of her in you. I'd just hoped that you took the

28

few good pieces she had. Did she tell you not to tell me where she's been? Of course, she did. Both of you bitches are in cahoots. Fuck you bitches. I just wanted to make sure everyone was ok. None of you visit me to see if I'm ok. Neither of you check to see if I'm living or dead. You send me away and put me in some big ass house by myself all the way in Milton. Y'all just want me out of your life, huh? Y'all are gonna burn in hell together! If you don't want to tell me where she's at, I will just wait here for her until she comes back. This is *her* house. The slut gotta come back sometime."

My grandmother gets her ignorant ass up and walks upstairs to her old room. She slams the door as if she has a good reason to be pissed. I'm still sitting in the same spot sipping on my mint tea. If this is an act, it's a damn good one. What was this crazy bitch up to? Why is she asking where my mother is? Why is she talking like she didn't ask to move to Milton in a big ass house? How the fuck does she think that she got to live in that house? She is living a privileged life because her daughter died. The daughter that she is so-called waiting here for. She must be lonely. If she wants to move back here, all she needs to do is ask. There is no need for her to go through all of this to move back in.

Things Start to Change

Claudia:

I wake up from a nap and can't figure out how I ended up back into my old room. It's like I'm losing time. I try to back track and search my mind for an explanation. I have no idea how I got here or why I am here. Shit's really foggy. Since I'm here, I start to look through my dresser to see if I want to bring anything back home with me.

Most of all my old things are still in this room. My granddaughter Karma purchased all new things for me to take to my new home so I ended up leaving most of my old stuff here. Who wants old shit when you can have new shit? I open the top drawer that holds my lingerie. I'm suffocated by the strong smell of perfume. It smells like I spilled a bottle of perfume in there and just left it to sit. I stare at the contents inside.

Right beside my black suede toy bag is a glass jewelry box. *How in the hell did these get in here?* Inside of my jewelry box is all the jewelry that I swore the cleaning lady stole. I was ready to cuss her ass out over this jewelry. I was positive that she had stolen them. Well, I'm glad that I found them. I would have felt really stupid accusing her of stealing my jewelry and then finding it in my own drawer. It was like someone was trying to play a sick joke on me.

What really worries me is that I still can't figure out how I ended up back here. I remove all my jewelry out of my jewelry box. I leave the box in the drawer because it reeks of perfume. I put all my pieces inside of my pocketbook. As I sit at the end of the bed, I look at the gray walls. What the fuck is going on with me? Whose idea was it to paint these walls a depressing gray? This room should be yellow. Yellow makes you smile. It is a cheerful color, hopeful color. I walk back to the drawer and take out all my toys from inside of the suede black bag. Again, I

31

leave the bag inside of the drawer because it stinks like perfume. It's so powerful of a scent that I start to feel a headache coming on.

I open the bedroom door and head down the hallway. All the lights are out like someone's trying to save electricity. I flip on the light so that I can see. *She ain't hurting for cash that bad that she needs to conserve electricity.* Now that the hallway is illuminated, I can find my way to the stairs without holding on to the walls for direction. I can see Karma prancing around in a tank top and panties like nobody but her ass is in the house. No fucking respect these young bitches have these days.

I'm now at the bottom of the stairs and she looks at me for a split second then continues with the phone conversation she's having. She's a hoe just like her mama. I hear the shit she's saying on the phone. I can't tell if she's talking to a man or a woman. You never know with her confused ass. As I am walking to the kitchen island, I can hear bits and pieces of her conversation. Did she just tell someone that they better masturbate before she gets there because she won't tolerate a non-stamina having man? She said she needs three rounds or it's not worth the trip.

She gets her boldness from me. I'm almost proud of her. Back in the day when I was doing my thing, I talked all types of shit. Men are attracted to confident women. Confidence comes easy when you look as good as I do. Unfortunately, the only man that I truly loved, didn't love me. From then on, I used men to get what I wanted. I may be in my seventies, but I can hang with bitches in their late fifties. That's how I pulled my husband. He thought he was getting a young chick. I lied to him and said that I was fifty--eight. He believed me. To this day, I don't know if he knows my real age.

My husband, the minister, got locked up for embezzlement. I knew he was doing something shady, but I didn't care as long as he was getting money. I never planned on him getting caught. Once he got locked up I distanced myself from him. I visited him a few times, but that shit gets old quick. I'm in my seventies. I got no business visiting my man in prison.

Ava was always good at reading people. She could decipher fact from bullshit in a minute. When I told her that I was marrying the minister, she knew that my intentions weren't genuine. I never owned up to it, but I didn't have to. She knew what was up. I played my part and my position. He got caught and all our assets were frozen. I ended up having to come live with her to get back on my feet. Nobody wants to have to start thinking about generating an income once they are in their seventies. I should have been set by this age. Messing around with the minister got his money and my money taken.

I never had a good relationship with my daughter. I treated her like a stepchild her entire life. I was really upset with her father. She just got the heat. She's a much better person than I am for taking me in. If I was her, I would have told me to beat it. That must be from her daddy's side of the family. Her maternal side of the family is full of crazy motherfuckers that lack compassion. Her cousin, Craig, is one of them. He was somebody that you didn't want to mess over back in the day. He's grown into an even scarier person. All this talk about Ava, has got me wondering where she is.

I wonder if she went on a vacation or something. She's been known to dip out without telling anyone her whereabouts, but she never stays too long. I haven't seen or heard from her in a while. I'm almost starting to worry about her. She's trained my granddaughter well. She's all tight lipped. She won't disclose any information. If I'm anything, I'm patient. I will wait on Ava to get back. If she takes too long, I'll just have to do some investigating. Until then, consider me moved back in. I have enough clothes here that I don't need to go back to my house for at least three weeks. Let's hope Ava shows her ass before then.

Karma:

My grandmother is still here. She's acting like she's staying for a while. Last night she was ironing out her clothes for the week as if she had to go to work or something. I made several phone calls before I went out last night and she was ear hustling the entire time; so, I took my conversation upstairs to my room. Not because I was worried about her overhearing my conversation, but solely because she was irritating me.

She still hasn't said why she is here. Why she felt the need to sleep over is beyond my knowledge. She's definitely Ava's mother though. This morning, I walked past her room and heard her playing with her toys. She wasn't being discreet about it either. She knew that I was in the house. She just didn't give a fuck. If she still wants the dick in her seventies, I know I'm going to be just as bad as her, if not worst.

I stayed out all night. First, I went by to get my three rounds in with school boy. School boy is one of the three men from my roster that I call on to meet my sexual needs. I call him School boy because when we met he was in college. I usually don't fuck with boys still in school, however, School boy is the exception.

When I talked to him last night, he said that he just came back from his basketball game. He had to play the entire game without having a sub. He whined that he may not have enough energy for three rounds with me tonight. I cussed his ass out and told him that be better not call me for some pussy if he can't go three rounds. He's young. Lack of stamina shouldn't ever be a part of our conversation. I asked him if this was going to be something that I should worry about. He said that I had no need to worry and to come through.

I don't know what he did, but he had no problem going the three rounds while I was there. After I left his house, I decided to head out and grab a drink somewhere. It was only 10pm and I had no desire to go home and deal with my grandmother's weird ass. I found myself at some club in the B.U. area. All the college kids were out enjoying themselves. I don't even remember the name of the damn club I entered. It was definitely jumping when I arrived. I pay the cover and head straight to the bar. The old-school song, "One More Chance" by Biggie is playing. The beat is hypnotic. I'm shaking my ass waiting on my drink order. Next thing you know, a large gentleman is dancing behind me at the bar. *Who does that?*

Usually, I don't play that. This time I let it play out. I wanted to know more about this man that was bold enough to take me from behind. I don't turn around. Instead, I decided to fuck with him to see where his mind was at. So, I let him dance with me and grind all up in my butt with that healthy hard on of his. If I was wearing panties, they would've definitely been wet. I drank my brown liquor and danced with this guy for three songs. When we stopped dancing, I still don't turn around to see who he is. I could feel him standing here waiting on me to turn around. I wanted him to be confused. I never turned around. I finished my brown liquor and ordered another. Eventually, he leaves.

Once I know that he is gone. I turn around. I'm not worried about trying to figure out who it was that I was dancing with. I know enough about men to bet my life that he would come back over to me before the night was over and reveal himself to me. In the meantime, I dance to

35

a few songs with other patrons and enjoy my night. I had two glasses of Hennessey and I was

starting to feel it. I told myself that I was going to leave my car there and call a cab home. Then I

thought about it and quickly talked myself out of that idea. I was not leaving my whip behind.

I didn't need a cab anyway. Just as I expected, Mr. Healthy Dick revealed his identity and

attempts to see what is up with me. Although, I'd just done three rounds in the sack with School

Boy, I was ready for some more. We went back to his place and fucked until exhaustion. This

man was bigger than most of the men I've dealt with, but I had no complaints. He was about six

foot one and roughly 275lbs. He was built like a football player. He told me his name. I think he

said it is Mike. I was really fucked up, so don't quote me on it.

From what I can remember, it was a really good night; a fulfilling night. I'm glad that I

stopped by that club and met some more dick. I may be adding Mike to the roster. He handled

me like I weighed ten pounds. His dick is thick. I almost had to brace myself. When I say that he

felt good; I mean his dick felt like it was tickling every nerve up in my pussy. I kept squeezing

my pussy walls to strangle the dick. He'd pump and I'd squeeze. He'd pump faster and I'd

squeeze harder. My pussy fell in love with his dick for the night.

What's vague is how we went from using a condom to not using a condom. I'm positive

that we started off with one. However, we didn't end with one. I'm not trying to die over dick. I

don't know this man to feel safe enough to go raw with him. I'm not worried about pregnancy,

because I learned my lesson and take my pills religiously. What I am worried about is where this

man's dick has been. If he went up in me raw without knowing me, I'm sure this isn't his first

time. Now, I'm going to have anxiety for a week. There's nothing like waiting on an HIV test.

All the questionable people and things that you've done haunt you. Fucking around with this man has made it a must that I get tested. I will schedule an appointment at my GYN's office for next week.

While he is sleeping, I leave his apartment. I don't leave my number. I don't leave a note. I just bounce. As I walk in the parking lot towards the visitor's spot, I replay last night's events in my head. I had a good night. If he plays his cards right and didn't give me a sexually transmitted disease, I might come back and see him with a value size box of Magnums in my purse.

It's 4 A.M. I'm sitting in my parked car gathering my thoughts. Jill Scott's Wild Cookie is playing. It's dark outside. I have my headlights off with my car running. I'm still a little fucked up. I'm trying to gage how fucked up I really am. Can I make it home without killing myself or someone else?

Just as I turn on my headlights, I see a woman that got it in all the right places. She's walking towards my car. I'm wondering how this is going to play out. She's obviously coming to my car. Just in case she thinks of some dumb shit -like try to rob me -I reach under my seat for my gun. Ava taught me how to use a gun. She also told me to never pull it out unless I wasn't afraid to use it.

I don't feel like getting robbed and killed tonight. So, I pull my gun out from under the driver's seat. I roll my tinted window down and have the gun aimed right at her pussy in case she needs more than directions.

"Whoa! Wait! Don't Shoot!" she yells.

"What the fuck do you want from a stranger at 4AM?"

"I'm usually turning tricks at 4AM, but tonight one of them beat the shit outta me."

I look at her and can see she's in pain. Her face is fucked up too. I didn't notice this when I was checking her out from afar. *Did she just say she's usually turning tricks?*

"What can I do for you?" I say with less of an attitude.

"Listen, I know that you don't know me and I know this feels shady to you, but could you please bring me to the emergency room? I'm hurt."

My instincts are telling me to keep that gun in my right hand and drive off with my left. I size her up and see if I can take her if some shit jumps off. The closer I look at her, the stronger she looks. That's when I conclude that this bitch isn't a bitch at all. She's a man. Shit is getting really interesting now. I decide to take a risk.

"You do look like you're in a lot of pain. Hop in. I'll bring you to Boston Medical Center."

I'm still fucked up. I know it. I shouldn't be driving. She, or should I say he, hops in. I ask her name and she says "Joan."

"Formerly Joe or John?" I ask.

She looks at me and smiles, but says nothing. Sixty seconds into the drive she says

"Look, I just escaped death. I'm not trying to let you kill me. Let me drive."

"You ain't driving my whip" I snap as I swerve out of the way of the sidewalk that seemed to just appear in front of the car. When she asks me to let her out, I realize that I may need to reevaluate the risks. We are more at risk of me killing us both than her trying to get over on me and do something shady.

I pull over because common sense is telling me to get the hell out of the car and let Joan drive. She gets out too. We silently switch spots and she drives. I now feel like I'm going to throw up. I guess the Hennessey finally caught up with me. As soon as I start to tell Joan that I feel sick, I puke all over the passenger side dashboard and front window. That shit flew out of my mouth like the exorcist. Miraculously, my vomit missed the heating vents and speakers. Thank God for small blessings. My car would smell like vomit indefinitely if it seeped into the vents.

I feel like shit. Joan is driving and not saying a word to me. She began driving again as soon as I finished vomiting. She doesn't even wait for me to clean it up. She doesn't ask if I am ok. I look at her. She's in pain. I realize that I haven't asked her if she's ok. I'm wondering what exactly happened to her. Before I know it, we are parked on Mass Ave near BMC. She gets out the whip, opens my car door and tells me that I'm coming with her. She says for my safety; she isn't giving me my keys. So, I can sit in my car without my keys or go with her. I decide to go inside with her.

Joan checks in at the front desk to wait to be seen while I take a seat in the waiting area. Instead of sitting beside me, she sits across from me. It feels like she doesn't want to be associated with me. Then again, I could be reading her wrong. I am drunk. We must have missed the rush. There are only two other people in the waiting area with us. I'm hoping this goes by quickly. I really just want to go home and pass the fuck out.

Thirty minutes later we are in the room with the intake person. I'm in the room with her because I'm nosey and she didn't object. Joan definitely fooled the intake person because once he gets to the box where it asks sex, he tells Joan that she mistakenly marked off male. Joan tells him that it is not a mistake. There is an uncomfortable pause. The intake person's demeanor

39

changes instantly. In a matter of seconds, he grew an attitude. He is pissed. I'm guessing that he is probably mad because he is attracted to her.

She is bad. Joan looks like Boris Kodjoe's wife Nicole Arie Parker. I don't know if that was on purpose or a coincidence. Joan could be her twin, except she has a bigger booty. And a penis. I could see how the intake person would be attracted to her. This intake worker is visibly tense. He now treats Joan cold and has a poor bedside manner. Anyone with eyes can see that somebody whooped her ass. She is in pain. He could care less. Joan seems numb to his bullshit. He is bothering me way more than it appeared he was bothering her.

He finishes taking all her information and tells us to be seated back into the waiting area until a nurse can see her. Twenty minutes later, she is seen by a nurse and sent home with some prescriptions. I didn't go into the ER with her. When she returned patched up, I didn't ask her what the nurse said. We both silently walked to my car.

Joan unlocks the door with the remote and we both get into the vehicle. Same spots. Same places. She doesn't even ask where I live. Instead, she presses the navigation panel on my dashboard and finds the address marked home. I still feel like shit and I am dead tired. Next thing I know, it's a new day and I'm waking up in my bed.

At first, last night feels like a dream. Then I snap the fuck out of my fog and realize that it wasn't. I have a headache that is pounding, but only on the right side of my head. I'm trying to assess my current situation. I don't remember anything after Joan found my address inside of the GPS. Thankfully and unlike me, Joan left a note.

Thanks for taking a chance. You really helped me out last night. Drink plenty of water.

Joan

She left her phone number at the bottom of the note. This bitch left a thank you note like she got some pussy from me. I laugh to myself. Joan certainly is an interesting person. I can't say that I have any friends or acquaintances like her. I will admit, I am a little intrigued about her lifestyle. I will call her tonight and see how the hoe's doing.

Claudia:

My granddaughter is one nosey little bitch. I heard her stop at my door while I was trying to ignite an orgasm from my vibrator. I didn't give a fuck though. I wasn't stopping just because her creepy ass felt the need to listen. I know she gets hers; so why she's worried about me getting mine is a mystery. It's definitely time for a companion in my life. My husband is locked up. He ain't getting out to give me none before my funeral. There ain't no sense in waiting on his old dick.

I need me some young dick anyway. Not too young, but some sixties dick will do. Ava put me on to vaginal rejuvenation. I didn't want beef curtain coochie, so I went ahead and had the procedure. It did wonders. My coochie probably looks as good as my daughters. Speaking of my daughter, she still hasn't come home.

We may not have the best relationship, but I'm still her mother at the end of the day. Ava needs to be a better daughter. She acts like I don't exist. I guess he left me in that house out in

Milton to die. Shit. She hasn't come to check on me since I've been there. It's not like she has a man and wanted her privacy. There was no reason for her to move me out of the house. Who does that to their own mother?

I've decided that I'm going home. There is no sense in staying here waiting on Ava's hoe-ass to show up. She will show up sooner or later. When she does, she's going to get a motherfucking earful. Bitch.

***

I need some company. I need someone to dote over me. I need someone to make me feel good. I need some dick. In my quest to get some, I plan to see what's up at the Ebony Gala. I'm sure I can snag a ticket from someone. I'll call Craig. I know he can get me a ticket. Since I'm on a dick hunt, I only need one ticket. I won't be calling Rochelle to join me. I don't need another bitch trying to compete with me.

I look inside of my closet. There's nothing in it that I feel is sexy enough to wear. I'm going to have to take a trip to the mall. Nordstrom's should have something sexy for me. I'm coming home with a man tonight. I may need to buy some new panties and a bra too. I may be in my seventies, but I can give most fifty-year old women a run for their money. My family has good genes. That's why Ava and Karma's body looks so good. They have me to thank for that. Well, maybe not the genes. But, they can thank me for making sure that they knew the importance of keeping your body tight.

I come back from Nordstrom's with a beaded black V-neck dress. It's gorgeous. Its form fitting and stops right above my knees. I intended to buy a new bra and panties, but decided against it. I'm not wearing any panties tonight. I must say, my ass is looking right in this number. As I'm modeling in front of the mirror admiring my ass, I look at my bra-less titties. My titties will have the help of a push-up bra. Don't get me wrong. I still have nice titties, but a push up bra never hurt anybody. My titties need to look perky if I'm on the hunt.

Craig comes through, like I knew he would. One of his goons drops of my ticket. I open the door and let him in. My robe is on but it is untied and slightly open. He looks right at me as if it is normal for me to be walking around half naked. He goes inside of his pocket and hands me the ticket. As he hands me the ticket, I take it out his hand and rub his now free hand over my nipple. He doesn't even flinch. Neither one of us say anything. I do that to see if he is down. The way that he is looking at me, I can tell he is.

I take his hand and slide it down my stomach and I lead him to the heat I have down below. Craig's goons all look good. I don't know how old this one is. Shit, I don't even know his name. What I do know is that he's going to be eating this rejuvenated pussy up in a few minutes. Once I led him further down to my hot kitty, I could see his dick try to escape his jeans. I aid him in its attempt to escape.

I unbutton his pants and feel an eggplant. This shit keeps getting longer and thicker with each stroke I give him. God has truly blessed me. This man is going to leave a dent in my shit. We are both giving each other hand jobs but I grow impatient. I am ready to get down to business. I order his ass to get on his knees. He smiles and does as he is told. Then I smack him dead in the face. He's stunned. I don't give him a chance to react. I pull his head to my pussy and order him to lick it clean. I have on my heels. I'm at the perfect height for him to eat my pussy right. And he does just that.

43

I'm not a selfish lover. I inhale his dick. I slobber all over it. His dick takes up most of the space in mouth. When I sucked dicks in the past, I usually had some space for breathing; not today. Once my mouth adjusts to his thickness, I make sure he is swollen to his full potential. He is feeling my head game. I can tell because he keeps trying to gag me. I am ready to see what this dick can do.

We fuck on my expensive travertine kitchen floor. We are like two nasty sexual beasts. The shit is good. I'd been in heat and he is putting in that work. When I cum, I cum hard. He came after me. He makes no sound at all, but the facial expression he wears gives it away. It looks like he is trying to shit and is constipated. I have to shut my eyes because the ugly face he is making is turning me off.

When his heart rate slows down some, I get off him and walk towards the bathroom. As I walk away, I tell him to let himself out. There is no need for hospitality. We both know what's up. This is just a fuck. I need to take a shower and get ready for the Ebony Ball. I'm looking for some steady dick tonight, not some goon dick.

The Ebony Ball is a sea of black and brown sophisticatedly dressed people. Although, not everyone is dressed right. There are a few hoes in here that have on shit that is too tight and too cheap for my taste. One hoe, in particular, has a whole bunch of shit wrong with her outfit. The first thing that I notice is that she clearly isn't wearing any panties. She has on winter white slacks that are high waters. The pants fit like spandex in the crotch area highlighting her camel toe. The back of her ass has a sweat stain as if she's been working out at the gym. Her shirt is just as bad. It is a fake leather wrap shirt with a sequined collar. It is too small. The cleavage effect that she is giving is like a size D cup size trying to squeeze into an A cup. It is just too much. I'm not even going to start in on her shoes.

I take my attention off this lost cause and scan the room for steady dick. I see a few potentials so I make a mental note of where they are standing and what they are drinking. Before I begin my hunt, I head back to the bar to grab a glass of red wine and listen to some music. As I'm enjoying my wine, this one man catches my eye. He looks to be in his late fifties or early sixties. His suit is tailored. His shoes look expensive and his watch is low key, but an expensive low key. It's the type of watch that people with real money recognize, but others would mistake for something inexpensive because it is not flashy. Something about him seems familiar. I need to get a closer look.

I keep my eye on him, while I finish my drink. When I'm done, I walk over in his direction. On my way, over to him, a nice-looking guy approaches me. I try to show him some attention, without taking my eye off the other man. I manage to get his name and number. I'll get to know him later. Right now, I'm set on getting a good look at the mystery man. Before I can get to him, another woman, pulls him away and I get stopped by another potential looking to see what I'm about. I'm pissed off because the mystery man is nowhere to be seen. He must have left. I decide to turn my attention back to this man spitting game at me.

He talks too damn much. As he is talking about himself, I'm thinking about texting the first guy that I met and asking him to come over to the table that I'm sitting at with motor mouth. Thankfully, as I'm contemplating how I'm going to exit this conversation, he excuses himself to the restroom. He says that the beers are going right through him. Finally, he's gone. As I stand up from the table to leave, I feel a man's hand at the small of my waist. I turn around and I'm staring into a set of caramel brown eyes. It's the mystery man. It's Ava's father.

"It's been a long-time Claudia."

"Is that how you greet the mother of your child that you haven't seen in damn near fifty years? I'd say it's been more than a long time. It's been a damn life time." I say with an attitude.

"Come on now Claudia, you can't still be upset with me after all these years. Don't tell me that you're a bitter woman. If I know you, you got a replacement dad for our daughter soon after I stopped dealing with you."

He doesn't know me at all. "Whether I got a replacement or not, that doesn't take away from the fact that you abandoned your black family for your white one. You missed your first born entire life. I thought for sure that you'd come to your senses and at least seek out a relationship with your daughter. We both know THAT never happened. And yes, I've been angry ever since. You know, Ava looked just like you before the surgeries."

"Before the surgeries. What surgeries?"

"It's a long story. Never mind that; What are you doing here?"

"I've been coming to this event for years. When I divorced my second wife, I needed to clear my head. A friend of mine invited me to this event and I've been coming ever since."

"Your second wife? You mean to tell me that you left your first wife and didn't look me up. Your no-good ass didn't check on us. You just went and built another life with another white woman and that marriage didn't last either?"

"She isn't white. She's black."

"That makes it even worse! I really can't handle this conversation right now. It is making me experience all types of emotions. Listen, it was nice seeing you again. Actually, it really wasn't. I gotta go."

I walk away. I need another drink. The man that I loved and wanted to marry was standing in front of me and acting as if what he did was no big deal. I'm back at the bar and before I know it, working on glass number six. I am ready to go home. I'm tore up.

Ava's no good daddy makes his way over to me. Next thing I know, I'm at my new house in Milton riding an old pink penis. I honestly don't remember anything up to this point. I look at this elderly white man making an ugly face as he is getting ready to come. Like the bitch I am, I abruptly stop riding him and jump up off of his Porky Pig colored dick. He ain't getting anything else from me. I'll be damned if he gets a nut off.

"What are you doing? I was almost there!"

"You need to be almost out of my house! How dare you slide your old dick inside of me after all these years. You clearly took advantage of me because I'm fucked up. "

"Still a bitch after all these years I see!"

"A bitch? You know something? I'll let you have that. I am a bitch. I'm a bitter bitch that wants nothing to do with your ass. Get the fuck outta my house you deadbeat!"

"Your friend Rochelle didn't think I was a deadbeat when she was sucking my dick!" he yells as he is halfway out of the door.

He had me with that one. I didn't say anything. My instincts took over. It was as if somebody else took over my body. Next thing I know, I am throwing my high heel shoe at his head. Luckily for him, he is quicker than I expected. My shoe misses his head and lands right on the back of his neck.

He's stunned by this. "You Black Bitch!" he yells and then turns to run back towards me. I'm always ready for some craziness to go down. I got something for his ass under my fake tissue box that sits on my night stand. This fool actually runs towards me like he's going to beat me or something. As soon as he gets close, I take out my stun gun. I thought I was going to get a chance to use it, but he stops dead in his tracks. He is so mad. His face is crayon red. I look at him daring him to come closer. He slowly backs away. I guess he is making sure that I don't throw anything else at him. He makes it to the door.

"Tell that bitch Rochelle, that I got something for her ass if she ever shows her face around here again!" The door slams and my picture of Malcolm X falls off the wall to the floor. I head to the bathroom to wipe his residue off my coochie. The dog went up in me raw. I'm feeling the need to douche.

Joan:

Women wonder why they can't get a man. Wax your mustache. Shave your arm pits and your legs. Keep your weave neat and wear clothes that flatter your figure. I walk by a bunch of angry raggedy looking women all the time. I just shake my head. If God made me a woman, I'd bask in my femininity and celebrate everything that makes me a woman. These chicks are ungrateful.

Unless you are just like me, you have no idea what it feels like to feel like a woman, but have the anatomy of a man. My life has been such a contradiction. I feel like a hostage. Luckily for me, when I started to accept the real me, my mom did too. Not everyone has that story. My mom, bless her soul, was a straight shooter.

"Jonathan…you been in my clothes again?"

"Uh no."

"I didn't raise any liars! I know that you've been in my clothes. They smell like you."

"I'm sorry Mom" I say embarrassed.

"Be sorry for lying. Never be sorry for who you are."

"So, you know…you know about Joan?"

"Oh! Is that her name?"

"Yes mom, that's my name."

"Well, Joan, I enjoyed my time with my son Jonathan. It's now time that I get to know my daughter Joan. Let me just say this. I'm your mother. I love you unconditionally. Don't expect the world to lovingly embrace you. As a matter of fact, expect them not to embrace you. You will have some battles to fight. There are some very opinionated ignorant ass people in this world. Hopefully, you don't run across too many of them. But if you do, keep your cool. Don't let them see that they've gotten to you. Walk away from the situation because it's bound to be emotionally charged. But if you can't walk away because they are trying to intimidate you or hurt you physically; make sure you keep enough of Jonathan around to beat their ass!"

I'll never forget that conversation. My mom was my best friend. She was my confidant. She died in a car accident. She was killed by a drunk driver. I've felt so alone since she's been gone. It's only been a year, but it feels like forever. There is nobody as loving, strong, supportive, intelligent and resilient as my mother. She was such a beautiful soul. I miss her so much.

When I was in Karma's car, all I could think about was my mom. I wasn't going to let Karma do to someone else, what was done to my mom. I know I had no right to take her keys from her. After all, it's her car and it's her life. My objective was to keep her safe from herself and keep other drivers safe from her drunk behind. I wish somebody took the keys out of the hand of the drunk driver that killed my mother. She'd be here today.

Karma's must have heard me talking to myself about her. My phone is ringing and I don't recognize the number. When I answer, it's her.

"Hello?"

"Hi. Is this Joan?"

"Yes, it is."

"It's Karma… from the other night."

"I'm well aware of who you are."

"Ok good. So, you wanna have dinner or go out for drinks? My treat."

"I'll pass on the drinks, but dinner sounds like a plan."

"Ok good. So, I'll meet you at Cathay Pacific in Quincy tonight at 8pm."

"This sounds like a cheap date. You're gonna need to step it up and pick me up for that matter. You can pick me up at 7pm and we can go to the Cheese Cake Factory in Cambridge. I love that place."

"Uh Joan…do I look like your motherfucking man? I'll pick you up. Don't try to run game on me like I'm some trick."

"Aren't we sensitive this afternoon. Will you grant me a do-over?"

"Go right ahead."

"I would be honored to accompany you to dinner. If it is ok with you, my palate thoroughly enjoys the Cheese Cake Factory. Could we dine there this evening? Would it also be ok if you picked me up? I'm without any transportation" I sarcastically say.

"Damn Bitch, all that tricking and you don't have a car. You either ain't hustling hard enough or ain't charging enough. Geesh! I know you ain't got no pussy but we gonna have to work on that head game. If you're good, I'll demonstrate on you."

"I knew you had issues when we met, but now I see I've underestimated just how many you have Karma."

"Whatever. Text me your address and I will pick you up at 7pm."

She hung up the phone not waiting for me to say ok or say goodbye. I texted her my address. She replied. *I'm not getting out the car. Look for a navy-blue Infiniti SUV.*

Karma:

Joan must've thought I was one of her tricks. I invited her out to dinner and she tried to boss me into picking her up and going to a spot she picked. She had no clue who she was dealing with. I'm Ava's daughter. She has balls, literally and figuratively. I like that about her. Joan is interesting and she has definitely peaked my interest.

I hang up with Joan and start flipping through some hair magazines. As I'm flipping through, I see a cute picture of this chick. She was dark skin with a natural hairstyle. For a quick second, I thought about going natural. Then I thought about how consistently rough natural hair looks and the upkeep. I'm going to stick with relaxers until my scalp tells me to stop. I ain't about that nappy life. My hair needs to move when the wind blows.

I don't know why, but suddenly I get the urge to hear from Richard. I told myself multiple times that I would not call Richard. I just had an abortion because I was fucking around with him. I need to leave well enough alone. but I don't. Putting the magazine down I dial his number.

"Hello" Richard answers on the first ring.

"How about I buy you a ticket, so you can suck on these titties of mine"

"When" is all that he says.

"Tomorrow" I say with a grin on my face.

"I can only stay for two days" he tells me.

"That's enough time for me to wear you out" I say with a hint of arrogance.

"Text me my flight information and you make sure your mouth, pussy and ass are ready for this dick; and in that order. As a matter of fact, send me a picture of all three; so, I can get my shit off in your absence."

"Damn, you want me that bad huh?"

"Always."

"Well you're gonna have to wait for it. You ain't getting no naked pictures of me to blackmail me with someday. You got good dick, but it ain't that good that I lost all my motherfucking common sense. You make sure you come directly to my house once you land. All three body entrances will be ready for you."

I hang up the phone, without giving him a chance to respond. I then pack my bags and head over to the condo I bought that nobody knew about. My mom thought that I was wasting my money on buying bags and clothes, but she should've known better. She taught me better than that. I bought my condo a month before she passed away. I never got a chance to tell her. I wanted to show her, but not before I had it fully furnished and to my liking. Never would have imagined she wouldn't be here.

The condo is where I planned on moving to in order to get away from my mother and grandmother. I needed my own space. Both of them are nosy as hell; I didn't need them tracking who came in and out of my bedroom so a new place to call my own was necessary. Originally, I thought that I was going to be married and living with Ray, but that shit didn't happen. So, I had to resort to Plan B which was to obtain my own piece of real estate. Like I said, I told nobody about it, not even Eve.

I'm entering the I90 tunnel when I remember that I have a bright orange envelope sitting on my dresser. It's been there for a week and I haven't opened it. I know what it says. I've gone over my prepaid balance and I need to put money back into the EZ Pass account. It's not like I don't have the money, I just never feel like listening to the twenty prompts that it takes to pay the shit over the phone. Some time tonight I'll make time to pay it.

Once I hit the toll I fly through--instead of slowing down--not wanting to see the light turn red. I'm used to it being yellow which indicates that I have a low balance. I'm positive that I don't have a low balance. I have no balance. I know all it's going to be is a fine. I got the money to pay it, but for some reason as I fly through the toll, I get that uneasy feeling you get when the police are behind you. EZpass isn't pimping me. I didn't sign up for automatic withdrawals. I don't like the idea of that. I don't care if it is two dollars, I'll pay you when I'm ready to pay you.

There's a sea of red brake lights in the tunnel. I'm in no mood for traffic. The driver that is stopped in front of me has her window down and her left arm is hanging out of the car with a nasty cigarette. With my windows, down, it's like I can smell the cancer being blown out of the cigarette. I was trying to enjoy the fresh air but that shit ain't happening. I'm in this hot ass claustrophobic tunnel and this bitch is polluting the already polluted tunnel air.

I can't stand the smell of cigarette smoke. This bitch is straight disrespectful with it too. As I roll up my window, I give her an exaggerated dirty look. She sees me in her driver's side mirror and we lock eyes. As if out of spite, she blows smoke from her mouth out of the window, then gives me the finger. I'm pissed and ready to go off. Not wanting to act like a fool, I have a serious talk with myself for about four long seconds. That's all I needed for myself to say "whoop this bitch's ass!"

I open my door and walk over to her car. When she notices me, she starts rolling up her window. The window ain't quick enough. I splash the water from my Poland Springs bottle on her cigarette as the window is automatically rolling up.

"You fucking black bitch!" the Hispanic chick screams.

I look at her like she's crazy. She's got a fucking nerve; I'm lighter than her, at least two shades. Without saying anything in retaliation, I walk back to my car. She got my point and the cigarette was out. All is well in my world. I wasn't afraid that she was going to retaliate because if she was, she would have jumped out of the car by now. If I was her, when I saw me coming, I would have slammed open the driver's side door to hit me with it. Obviously, that bitch ain't me.

I get back into my car and put on "Golden", an old-school jam, by Jill Scott. With the music blasting, I sing the song like I'm at Jill's concert. Through her rearview mirror, I can see that Hispanic bitch giving me dirty looks. I'm not phased. Like I said before, if she was going to do something, she would have done it. She ain't about that life. Instead, she stayed her pastelito eating ass in the car like she had sense. Traffic begins to move and I'm out of the tunnel in five minutes. She goes her way and I go mine. Once the tunnel splits, I hear her beep her horn all extra-long. That was some punk shit.

Eve:

I have my plan C. I'm going to stay in Charlotte until I figure things out. I don't want to go broke living at this hotel and still pay rent in Boston so I decide to look into renting an apartment ASAP. Using my phone, I look online to find a reasonably priced apartment; however, I can't find anyone willing to lease an apartment for a six-month span. Everyone wants you to sign a year lease. *Fuck it.* If I decide to leave early and break the lease, I'll deal with that when the time comes.

If I'm going to stay here for at least six months, I need to find a job. I'm not trying to blow all my severance pay by not working. Now that I have my GED and experience working at Still Bitter Private Investigating Agency, I can get a job somewhere other than the minimum wage jobs I worked in the past. With the exception of killing Cynthia, I've come a long way in less than a year. I'm proud of myself.

I head down to the business center located on the first floor of the hotel. The elevator smells like a fart. I'm grossed out and hoping that nobody gets on the elevator before I make it to the lobby. You know if someone gets on, they will think that it was me that farted. I hate when people set you up like that. I call it being set up for the drive by. Nobody gets on the elevator.

My plan is to apply for at least ten jobs, wait a few days, then see if anyone bites. If nobody bites, I'll do the same thing every few days until someone does. This reminds me of when I was applying for the Boston job. I hope I have that same good luck and land a well-paying job. Working for Ava was the best job I've ever had. It's really sad that she's gone. They still haven't figured out who killed her. The cops may want to start with Craig. He's good for killing people's family; I wouldn't put it past him to kill his own.

While I'm on the hotel computer applying for jobs, this overweight black woman with her hair corn-rowed into a ponytail comes over. She looks way too old to be rocking that hair style. When she sits down at the computer next to me, I gasp and then hold my breath. This chick smells like straight ass. *Bitch, did you forget to wipe your butt?* I wonder if it is case of BV. I've had bacteria vaginosis a few times. My GYN said that whenever my PH is off, I can get BV. That can have you smelling like ass too.

Anyway, it's my personal opinion that you need to pay extra attention to your hygiene if you are severely overweight. She obviously doesn't share the same opinion. Living in Charlotte, I've met plenty of big girls who take care of their hygiene. Just because they are big doesn't mean that they can't make an effort to smell good. This chick is giving big girls a bad name. She disgusts me.

I can't handle the uninvited odor. I get up from the computer. I'm done anyway. As I walk away, I notice Ms. Dookie Bootie digging in her nose and then going right back to stroking the keys on the computer. I'm grossed out. It made me wonder who was using the computer before me and if they had any nasty habits like this chick.

When I say, she was digging in her nose, she was doing it like a stereotypical Asian. She had no shame. I walk over to the front desk before heading to the elevators. I tell the receptionist that she should get someone to wipe down the keyboards. She asks me if anything was wrong with my keyboard. I tell her that I have no idea if anything was on my keyboard, but the lady beside me was digging for gold without a tissue and went right back to striking the keyboard as if that was normal behavior. I walk away and leave it at that.

When I look back, I notice the receptionist putting on hand sanitizer. I push the elevator button with my knuckle to go back up to my room. While I wait, I watch the receptionist to see if she is going to make a call to housekeeping to wipe down the keyboards or do it herself. She does neither. I'm one of those people that reviews. You best believe that I'm writing a review of this place and I'm naming names.

As I exit the elevator, I see the housekeeper leaving my room. I have all my money on me so I'm not worried. Although there is nothing in my room of value to take, I don't trust anyone. And I wouldn't put it past anyone to steal. I know what it is like to really be down and out. I had to convince myself that going hungry was worse than stealing. Gina used to have me steal food from the grocery store when I was younger. It made me feel like the scum of the earth; I hated that I was stealing. What I hated even more was that I was part of a family that was broke.

When I'd complain to Gina that there was no food in the refrigerator, she'd tell me to go the grocery store and bring her something to cook if I was hungry. She never gave me money to buy groceries and she never went with me to the grocery store. When I first started stealing food, I'd steal stuff for her to cook for us. Once I caught on to the fact that I was the only one taking the risk, I stopped buying for us and only bought for me. She never said anything about it, but I figure it was because she wasn't hungry most of the time. She only had an appetite for drugs.

I became very skilled at stealing shit. I learned the exact time when lost prevention would change shifts. They didn't pay attention to the monitors as closely during that time. I'd also go with intent to steal when there were a lot of people shopping. The day before a holiday or the day of a big game was always ideal. Later, I became cool with one of the dudes in lost prevention and he would let me take shit without paying. Every now and then, I'd give him a hand job as a thank you. Thanks to Mr. Uncle, I became very skilled with providing sexual favors.

That was life for me. It was shitty. Stealing food is the least of my sins. At the point when I knew that Gina was too deep in her addiction to take care of me, I'd let Mr. Uncle hit it as long as the household bills got paid. I promised not to tell – he promised to keep the rent paid and the utilities on. He didn't know that I was too fearful of being placed in a foster home to tell. He could've gotten it for free, had he used that information against me.

I basically raised myself. Gina didn't get her act together until my later teenage years. It was after Mr. Uncle died that she got clean. By then, I was a full-fledged survivor. I didn't need her for anything. I'll admit, she tried to be somewhat of a mom and act like she cared enough about me - she would ask where I was going and when I was coming back - but that's as far as it went. Shortly after Mr. Uncle died, we both got jobs. The bills weren't going to pay themselves. Clean Gina wouldn't suck dick for money like Addict Gina would. Although I never wish death on anyone, I was glad when Mr. Uncle died. It gave my pussy a break from his old gray hairy dick. I don't know how old he was, but he was definitely older than Gina.

He was a nasty old man. He'd always go pee and not flush the toilet. I'd go into the bathroom after him and find foamy pee. When I was studying for my GED, I learned a few things by picking up random books in the library. One thing I learned is that you can tell a lot about someone from their urine. From what I remember reading, I think that Mr. Uncle must have had diabetes. According to the book I read, when your pee is foamy that's a sign that you got kidney issues. I never seen him watch his diet when he was at Gina's. He drank beer like it was water and ate greasy and sugary foods. He had to know that something was wrong with him. I guess he just didn't give a fuck.

Craig:

I don't put anything past anyone, that's why nothing surprises me. It was a bitch that ultimately killed Cynthia. I had a hidden surveillance camera in the hospital room. I watched the recording with Karma and a few members of my team. None of them recognized the bitch. I still don't know who she is or what reason she had to kill my lady. I do know that she had to know Karma--she used her name on the sign in sheet. The tape didn't have any audio. She talked to Cynthia for a good five minutes before she put some poisonous shit in Cynthia's IV.

I'm replaying the footage. Cynthia looks confused. Then she starts to cry. It's killing me to watch but I can't stop. I questioned if this is God's way of telling me that I don't deserve anyone good in my life. Just when I was about to put the game behind me, I'm forced back into it. I guess it's back to getting money and strengthening my empire. When I find the bitch that did this, it's a wrap for her and hers. The police still have no leads. I didn't tell them that I had video footage. I don't want them to find the chick that did this. She'll go to prison and I won't be able to personally torture her. I could have someone slice her up once she gets to prison, but I don't want anyone else to do this. I need to do this.

I wasn't there to witness the explosion, but I have nightmares about my cousin Ava getting blown up in Ben's car. I couldn't have known that Ava was going over to Ben's house. I also couldn't have known that she'd be in his car. The odds of both of those things happening were almost non-existent. I guess that's why people warn to never say never. I tried to figure out why Ava would be at Ben's and why she'd be in his car without him. Ben didn't die in a car explosion, Ava did. Ben was found poisoned and stabbed. There is a lot more to this story and the cops have no clue. But if there is one thing *I'm* good at, it's getting to the bottom of things.

Nothing Like Family

Eve:

What a difference a day makes. In this case, what a difference a month makes. I got my own place. I found Gina and she is living with me. I only have a one bedroom, but I have a sofa bed and for now, that's enough for her. She claims that she's clean and is committed to staying clean. I'm trying to handle her delicately so I haven't had a sit down with her yet. I want answers more than I want to make her feel bad about herself. Right now, I'm handling her with kids' gloves.

Two months ago, I would have never imagined I'd be living back in Charlotte with Gina. I landed a job at a staffing company as an administrative assistant. The pay is decent. It allows me to live without having to dip into the severance. So far, Gina has been on her best behavior. I don't think she knows what to make of me. The girl she knew was a drop out that worked a low wage job and partied every weekend. The new Eve has a place of her own, a job and a motherfucking GED. Once things settle down, I am definitely going to look into taking some college courses. Gina doesn't know this Eve. *I* barely know her; I'm just getting used to her, but I like her. I like her a lot.

I haven't received any more texts from that unknown number. I thought for sure that I'd hear from them again by now. They must want something. Why bother texting me if not? I know, they aren't interested in turning me in; because if so, they would have gone to the police by now. I'll just sit tight until I hear from them again. I can't imagine who it is that is texting me. They know that I killed Cynthia. What do they want from me? *Get it together Eve.* There's no sense in worrying myself about it. I'll hear from them soon enough.

Karma called me. She said that she was worried about me. She couldn't understand how I could just up and move back down to North Carolina. I assured her that I would be back, but I had some family business to get squared away before I could return to Boston. She said ok, but I could tell that she was disappointed. She told me that she was looking into becoming a motivational speaker. All I could say was "oh really!" *Who the fuck was she going to be motivating?*

Anyway, I keep our conversation short and sweet and tell her that I will talk to her next week. She makes me promise that I'll keep in touch once a week. It feels good to have someone that cares about you, but on the flip side, the stuff that I want to talk about with her, I can't. She'd never understand why I had to kill Cynthia. She'd judge me. I don't want to lose my sister, so I'll keep that info to myself.

There are three administrative assistants at the staffing company. One of them I talk to, the other I can't stand. The one that I talk to brings me hot chocolate every morning. Her name is Angel. She's so sweet. She's a little older than me, but only by a few years. We arrive to work early every morning. For the first fifteen minutes, we chit chat before folks start showing up. I am still new so I never have any gossip to contribute to our conversations. Angel always has shit to tell me. She's the admin for HR and has everyone's information. I am the admin for the headhunters. I have access to a lot of information, but it's limited to the applicants. Angel has access to the entire company's info.

Helen, the bitch I can't stand, does the same job that I do. We work in the same department. I was assigned to shadow her the first week. Once she showed me how to get into the company's portal and navigate the system, I no longer needed her. I learned a lot working for

Ava. There was nothing that this Helen chick could teach me after that; I still shadowed her though.

Fake recognizes fake. Helen is extremely fake. I know it because I'm also good at playing the fake game. The difference is, I play it and she is it. She's fake all day. I was curious to see if she was just fake for the sake of keeping her job or if she was fake off the clock too. To find out, I decide to invite her to lunch with Angel and I. Angel said she had too much work to do. I went ahead and asked Helen if she wants to go to lunch with me. I really want to give her a chance. This will be her opportunity to show me regular Helen instead of work Helen.

Her fake ass agrees to lunch so we drive to Nana's Soul Food restaurant. There are two Nana's locations. The office was closer to the Nana's near the airport. We wouldn't have been able to make it to the Nana's downtown. Since I don't have a car yet, she had to drive. She has a nice car. We are riding down the highway in a black Acura RDX. It's not an MDX, but she's not on an MDX salary. I plan on buying a car while I'm in Charlotte, which I will use to drive back to Boston, when I decide to go back. I'm not getting a luxury vehicle, but it will be better than that used Carolla I have parked at my apartment in Boston.

We are finally at Nana's and I'm starving. I order macaroni and cheese, greens, yams and fried chicken. She just orders vegetables. *How in the hell are you going to go to a soul food restaurant and not order soul food?* I already don't trust her. I already know that I don't like her, but, like I said, I want to give her a chance.

Helen takes chooses a table close to the wall and the exit. I take the seat facing the door while her seat has her back to door. She doesn't seem bothered by it. Unlike her, I have a few enemies here in Charlotte that I can't afford to not see coming in. When I first arrived in

65

Charlotte, I was asking around about Gina. People told me what they knew about Gina, but folks couldn't wait to tell me about Lynn. Apparently, Lynn still runs her mouth about me. Her cousin is supposedly going to track me down and beat my ass. I smile as I remember punching out her cousin's tooth.

Helen is talking to me while I'm thinking about Lynn's toothless cousin. She caught me smiling.

"Oh, so you're a Republican too?" she asks.

My facial expression goes from smiling to grimacing. "Republican? Hell no! What Black people are Republicans? I'll admit, back in the day, Black people supported Republicans because that party supported our interests. Lincoln was a Republican. That was way back in the day. Today, Democrats support our interests. Black people vote according to the issues not the party. We aren't loyal to a particular party. We support those that support our interests. Period. Republicans don't care about us."

"I'm a Republican" she says while she eats her vegetables.

"Well, I'm not and I honestly don't trust any Black people that are" I say with an attitude.

"Do you think that's fair Eve? Do you think it's fair to judge someone based solely on their party affiliation?"

"Yup." I say in a matter of fact manner.

"Well, would it be fair if I judged you on your affiliation?" she snidely remarks.

"Yup, go right ahead. I'm a Democrat and I'm proud of it."

"Hmmmm, ok, so, if I judged you based on you being the daughter of a local crackhead, would that be fair?"

Did this bitch just call my momma a crackhead? I know it's true, but that's not the point.

I cough. I actually choke a little because I was drinking lemonade when she said it.

"It certainly would. It should tell you that I'm a strong woman. I'm a survivor. I'm resilient."

"Is that so?" Helen says smirking.

I need my job. That's why I answered her with the "resilient" bullshit. I don't like that fucking smirk that she has on her face right now. I'm erasing that shit right now.

"You find something amusing Helen?" I don't wait for her to respond.

"You know what I find amusing? I find bitches like you amusing! Bitches like you are real quick to talk shit to people that you think are not your equals. You think you're better than me for some reason. For the life of me, I can't figure out why. Aren't you the same weak uterus having bitch that had three miscarriages this year? Is it because you were born like that? Nope. It's not because God made you that way. It's because your "Republican" pussy had to have three abortions in less than two years dealing with these White married motherfuckers at the office. Now, you found a Black man to love your rotten pussy having ass, but can't give him a baby. I saw him. He's a cutie. I've seen him check me out a few times on the low. Maybe he's ready for some good pussy. And believe me, I got some good pussy. If you keep fucking with me, I'll give him something he won't be able to refuse. Now think about that the next time you want to look down on somebody you "think you know". BIIIIITCH!"

She's ruined my lunch. That's what I get for trying to give bitches a chance against my better judgment. She gives me one of the evilest looks I've ever seen but says nothing. Then a tear runs down her cheek. For a minute, I feel bad. I walk away from the table. *Fuck that bitch.* I tap on my Uber app and arrange for a ride back to work. She sits there and finishes her vegetables in silence.

I arrive back at the office with ten minutes left of my lunch break to spare. I head right over to Angel's desk. She's eating an Italian sub and working at the same time. She asks me what happened to Helen.

"How'd you know something happened to Helen?"

"I know because she called here and said that she had a family emergency and can't return back to the office. That means that you are going to have to finish her assignments before end of day today."

"That bitch didn't have a family emergency. I cussed her ass out when she called my mother a crackhead. She's a smug bitch. She didn't even give us a chance to bond. She just went straight for the jugular. Helen didn't know who she was fucking with."

"Oh, My God! What did you say to her Eve?"

"All I said was that she should have used a form of birth control when she was sleeping with these married white guys from the office. I told her that she can't give her man a baby because she had so many abortions. I might have also threatened to push up on her man if she keeps fucking with me."

"You said what! Girl, I can't tell you anything! She's gonna know that I told you all that stuff now. In the future, if you are going to cuss somebody out, make sure you do it without mentioning shit I told you. Helen can report me to HR at the corporate office if she wants."

Angel is visibly pissed at me. I feel bad. I assure her that Helen won't report her. She'd be stupid to. Helen would be making herself look bad if she did that. On top of that, she'd be telling on herself and the men in the company she slept with. She wants her job. She ain't going to say shit. I can guarantee that. Angel now looks a little more reassured. I know that she needs her job. She's been good people. The last thing I'd want to do is jeopardize her bread and butter.

"That bitch deserved it!" Angel says and laughs.

"I believe that, but why do you say that?"

"Last year, I was fucking the Director of HR. She found out and threatened to report me. I need my job, so I stopped fucking with him. He didn't even fight me on it. I was surprised we ended things so easily. I later find out that Helen was fucking him too. She was in love with him though. I knew he was married and wasn't leaving his wife. Helen didn't. The Dummy thought that he was going to leave his wife for her. He ended up promoting me like he promised he would. That's why I got the admin job in HR. I was in your position before. Helen and I worked together. She's been bitter ever since I got the position and he stopped fucking her."

"Damn, this place is like a reality show or a soap opera. I definitely won't be fucking with any of these white men."

"You say that now." Angel laughs.

"Now and forever." I laugh with her.

Wait, how'd Helen know about my mother? Angel…

Karma:

I should be ashamed of myself, but I'm not. It's been a month since Richard visited me for the weekend. We never left the condo. That man has quite an appetite for sex. When he was eating me and then started to finger me simultaneously, I thought of Eve. I remembered her telling me that she loved it when he did that to her. I wish I could tell her so do I! Ray ain't got nothing on Richard! He could learn a thing or two from little brother. Let me rephrase that. He could learn a thing or two from his younger brother because ain't nothing little about Richard. I went back to my house after I dropped Richard off at the airport. The condo is my little getaway when I need a change of scenery, but don't want to go too far.

Joan's supposed to be coming over this morning. Ever since that day we met for dinner, we been as thick as thieves. That's my ace. It's like she picked up right where Eve left off. I'm slowly learning more and more about transgender issues through Joan. One night, after a few drinks, I tried to make a move on Joan. I like having sex with women and men. Joan was the best of both worlds. I asked her to show me her dick. She wouldn't show me.

I was disappointed, but I wasn't giving up. This time when she came over, I put my hand up her skirt and tried to feel her dick. She pushes me off her and asks what the fuck my problem is . I tell her that I enjoy sex. I like it *a lot*--more than a lot--and I want to have sex with her. She isn't with it. She says she's not into pussy. That amazes me because she has a dick. So, I ask her if she's gay. She then tells me it is a little more complicated than that.

"You want to get your operation and I want to fuck you. I think we can both help each other out."

"Oh yeah. How's that?" Joan asks.

"If you agree to have sex with me for one night, I will pay for your surgery."

"No. I'm gonna have to pass on that."

"So, you'll go out here and have sex with all these random men for chump change, but you won't have sex with me? You know I got the money. You told me that this surgery would solve a lot of your problems. You're going to turn down something that you've been dreaming about because you don't fuck with pussy? It can't be that important to you then."

Joan didn't say anything she just picks up her glass of wine and walks into the living room to watch reruns of Ru Paul's Drag Race. I know that I planted a seed. I might not be getting any dick tonight, but believe me; Joan will come around.

I follow Joan into the living room and act like we never had the conversation. As soon as I sit down on the couch, my doorbell chimes. It's the pizza that I ordered. I already paid online with my credit card. I take the pizza without giving a tip. All that I had was a twenty-dollar bill. I was going to ask the delivery man if he had change, but when I see him give Joan a disgusted look, I take the pizza out of his hands and slam the door in his face. *Fuck his tip.* They charged me an extra three dollars for delivery any way

I should have given him a pound, because he had perfect timing. I know the look that he gave Joan got inside of her head. He just helped my quest for trans dick without even knowing it. I don't like that he made Joan feel bad about herself, but I do know that she'll really consider sleeping with me now. I tell Joan that I have to get something out of my system so she can chill and I'll be back in an hour or so. I am tempted to call up BJ, but instead I call up School Boy. I'm sure he misses me by now; I haven't given him any in at least two weeks.

71

Joan looks at me as if she is wondering if I am really going to leave her in my house alone. She grabs her pocketbook and gets up to leave. She has a slight attitude. I'm wondering if the attitude is directed at me or if she's still mad at the delivery guy. She says nothing. As she is walking to the door, I tell her to hold up.

"Hey, I may be gone for the night. No sense in this pizza going to waste."

"Are you sure that I'm the only biological man in this room right now?"

"Why you say that?" I ask confused.

"Your behaviors are so much like a man. First you offer me money to fuck you. Then when I say no, you want nothing else to do with me. Let me guess…you're off to get some dick from someone else, huh? You couldn't just eat this fucking pizza with me and chill. You really got a problem Karma. I'm gonna fall back though."

She says all of this while she's walking to the door. When she is done talking, she snatches the pizza and slams my door. That shit was a turn on. I am definitely fucking Joan. She'll come around. We'll see just how bad she wants that surgery. I've been fucked by a woman with a dildo, but I ain't never had trans dick. This I must try.

Eve:

I wake up earlier than usual today. I decide to head into work and I arrive forty-five minutes early. Angel isn't here yet. The only people here are two security guards. The first guard looks to be somewhere around Gina's age, maybe fifty. His beard is gray, but the mini afro he's rocking is jet black. *I wonder if he dyes his hair.* He has a deep southern accent. The accent sounds like it's more southern than North Carolina.

His name is Joe. I know this because it is on his white name tag. Joe is the supervisor. At least that is what his name tag says. I show Joe my badge as I enter the building. He attempts to have a conversation with me. We've never spoken to each other.

"Good Morning Ms. Eve! You're here bright and early today. Big meeting or something?"

Damn, he's nosey. Well, I guess that IS his job. "Hi." I say without answering his question.

"Nice day out there this morning. Don'tcha think?"

Ok, I'm gonna try to be nice today and give him the small talk he's seeking.

"Yes, It's very nice out today. North Carolina weather beats Massachusetts weather any day of the week."

"Oh, you're from Massachusetts? The second guard cuts in. His accent tells me that he is from the North. Now he's talking to me.

"No. I'm from Charlotte. I have family up there."

"Word? I wonder if I know any of your people."

"I doubt it." I say as I'm pressing the up button to call the elevator.

"Well, Ms. Eve, if you ever want to have lunch or just some coffee, I'd be happy to join you. I'm new to the area and lunchtime gets a little lonely. By the way, my name is Greg."

"Yes, I know your name. It's on your name tag." Then the door to the elevator opens. I walk in and say nothing more. He's a cutie, but I have a bad taste in my mouth for those that work in security. Richard works in that field.

I get up to the 9th floor and nobody is here. It's dead quiet. I walk by Helen's desk. Her shits messy. She has papers all over the place. There's old coffee from the day before in the cup. She has house slippers that look like they've seen better days under her desk. They look like they stink; kind of like her breath. I'm not sure why, but when we first met, I thought she looked like her breath stank. It didn't, but she does have that nasty yuck mouth look.

Anyway, I am tempted to go through her stuff. This may be the only opportunity I get to see if she got something I can use against her if she wants to act up and try to do something that might cause me to lose my job. Temptation takes over and I start to look through her cabinets. None of them are locked. I figure it is because she left yesterday after our lunch date.

The cabinet has two doors that open up top; that takes up half of the cabinet. The other half of the cabinet is divided by three drawers underneath. I go to the bottom drawer first. I'm not sure why, but I find that most people put their personal shit in the bottom drawer. Personal shit is exactly what I find.

Am I really looking at toys? Ok, this chick is bugging. She has anal beads, a vibrator and a huge dildo at work. When does she have time to do that? I take a picture with my cell phone. That was all that I needed to see. If she has them at work, then that means that she's using them at work. It has to be after hours. I leave an ordinary looking black pen in a cup that she uses as a pen holder. There are so many pens in the cup that I doubt that she'll ever get to mine. It's in the perfect position to see everything. If it was my desk, I'd notice that there was a foreign pen on it. Her shit is so messy I doubt that she'll ever notice the pen.

Just as I sit down at my desk, in walks both Helen and Angel. Helen goes directly to her desk to put down her pocketbook. Then she heads to the coffee maker; hopefully, to get rid of that nasty cup of old coffee she had sitting at her desk. Angel doesn't go to her desk. She comes directly to mine. We usually shoot the shit at her desk. Her coming to my desk meant that she had some personal shit to discuss.

"What's up? Why do you look like you want to beat somebody down?" I say to Angel.

"My son's father thinks he's slick that's why!"

"Girl, you're yelling like I did it. Take it down a notch. What happened?

"So, you remember when I told you that he is supposed to be getting married to this chick he's been dealing with for the last three years. Well, he told me that he's not going to be able to pay me the same amount of money that we agreed upon when my son was born."

"Did he fall on hard times or something? Did he lose his job?" Angel looks irritated.

"No, that fool didn't fall on hard times. He's still making the same money. In fact, he's making more. He told me that he needs money for his wedding expenses and his honeymoon. He wants to pay me $500 a month instead of the $850 we agreed upon. Now, you know, if he lost his job or something, I wouldn't sweat him about it. That's not the case here. He makes more money not less, but he wants to pay me less. How does he expect me to live off that? That's a big cut. He's gonna take away from our son, to pay for a wedding with his new bitch. I don't think so. I'm not gonna fight with him though. Guess where I'm going during lunch today?"

"Where are you going Angel?" I'm thinking she's going to go find his fiancé and step to her. That's what I would have done.

"I'm going to file for child support. If he thinks he's going to marry some chick and forget about his son's needs, he's out of his fucking mind. I'm not going to let that happen. I bet he hasn't asked his other baby's mother is he can start paying her less. Shiiiiiit."

I don't have any kids and I've never been in this situation, but I can say that I'd try to work it out before involving the government. I don't tell her that. Instead, I tell her that I understand where she's coming from and I hope things get resolved soon.

Personally, I think that she's just jealous. She's been looking for love and hasn't found it. Her ex-man found love and she can't handle it. Common sense tells me that if he's been taking care of his son consistently all this time, he's not going to just stop because he's getting married. Weddings cost a lot of money. It sounds like he just needs to pay less while he gets his finances in order for the wedding. It didn't sound like a forever thing. It sounded like a temporary thing, but I'm just speculating. Angel leaves my cubicle and goes back to her desk. She has a bitter look on her face.

Helen walks by my desk. She gives me a dirty look, but says nothing. She better be glad I need this job or else I'd have jumped on her. She better watch herself. I laugh. She doesn't need to watch herself because I'm watching her now. I flash my pearly whites at her as she gives me the dirty look. This bitch will be gone soon enough. *Keep fucking with me Helen.*

"Enjoy your day Helen!" I say as she's walking away from my desk.

"I will!" She says in a fake white girl tone and gives me the finger.

***

Since she couldn't yesterday, Angel is supposed to have lunch with me today. I know that she is going to cancel on me again. She wants to go to the court house to get her son's father served with papers for child support. I arrive to work fifteen minutes early to catch up on Angel's saga. I swipe my badge and look up to find Greg grilling me. He doesn't say anything. He's just staring. I ignore him and walk towards the elevator. If he has something to say, he needs to just say it.

I enter the elevator and press floor nine. Just as the doors are shutting I hear my name being called. I know who it is. I act like I don't hear him. It's Greg. I know he is feeling me. He better get some balls. How are you going to be a security guard and act all scared and shit? He might want to rethink his choice of employment.

I expect to find Angel at her desk. She's not there. I sit in a cubicle that's positioned where I can see who is getting on an off the elevator. Each time the elevator door opens, I look up to see if it is Angel. Our shift starts in five minutes. That's not like her not to be early. The black republican arrived five minutes ago. The elevator door opens again. I look up and then look back down. *Shit, he's coming over to my desk.*

"Why you act like you didn't hear me call your name earlier?"

"Oh, that was you calling me?" I say with a smirk on my face.

"You got jokes huh?"

There's an awkward moment of silence. I take the opportunity to size him up. He's tall, muscular, dark-skin, broad shoulders, Caesar cut, dimples; I wonder what he's working with. He asked me a question that I missed because I was too busy checking him out.

"So, we good for lunch then?"

I obviously missed an important part of our conversation. I'm about to decline, but then I change my mind and agree to meet him for lunch. Angel walks out of the elevator with a minute to spare. Greg leaves. As he walks away, I see thirsty Helen checking him out.

"Hiiiiii Greg!" Helen sings. Greg turns around and smiles at her. He waves and enters the elevator. *I can't stand that bitch.*

This morning is super busy. Two major insurance companies are having a massive hiring. They reached out to our company to fill the non-entry level positions. We are one of the best staffing companies in the state. I remember when I looked for jobs during my lunch hour at Walmart. I'd come across jobs staffed by this agency often. I never fit the eligibility. That was before I had my GED and my work experience at Still Bitter Private Investigating Agency. A year later, here I am.

I've been thinking more and more about taking some college courses. If I do, I'll take them online or in Boston. Massachusetts is the mecca for higher learning. I don't know how long I'll be in Charlotte but I'll be here until I figure things out with Gina. Before I left for work this morning, she was up cleaning and jamming to some old school 1990's music. She told me that she wanted to talk to me. She said that she wasn't strong enough before, but she feels strong enough to now.

I was almost tempted to call out of work before she changed her mind. However, I haven't been at the job long enough to be calling out. After my three months are up, it will be a different story. Greg came back up on the floor to do rounds and remind me that we have a lunch date. I figured we'd just go upstairs to the cafeteria. Instead, he told me that we had reservations at Fridays. That was the only decent place close by that we could eat and come back on time for work. *Since when does Fridays take reservations?*

I told him that I'd meet him out front at noon. I didn't need him coming over to my desk for the third time today. I don't like folks all up in my business. Folks probably talk about me now. I don't need to give them anything extra to talk about. I haven't received any more texts from anyone claiming to know my secrets. Every once in a while, I think about what I did. I feel sorry for Cynthia. She was what they call a casualty of war; but it was a necessary kill. I hope Craig suffers. I'm thinking about all of this while I am on my way down the first floor to meet Greg.

"You look nice today" Greg says once I step off the elevator.

"Just today? Come on now. You and I both know that you are checking for me every day. You could probably tell me what I had on every day of last week. I know it's just not "today" that I look nice."

"I had no idea you were that full of yourself Ms. Eve."

"Yup." I say with finality.

"Well, I don't scare off that easily. You and that big head of yours …"

79

Did this fool just call me big head? "It must be a northern thang to be intimidated by a woman that has confidence."

"Oh, is that so?"

"Yup." I say again with finality.

"You sure got a lot of mouth."

"Yup. Is that going to be a problem?"

"No Ma'am! Ise be jus fine." He says with a southern slave twang.

We both crack up and walk to the next complex to have lunch.

Greg is good people. I'm glad that I had lunch with him today. I really had a good time. We have a lot in common. I don't know why I sat there and told him my business, but I did. I wasn't even drinking. He was just really easy to talk to. But don't get it twisted, he told me his business too. We both made ourselves vulnerable to each other. It felt good to open up and just keep it real and it was refreshing to not feel judged. We are going to have lunch again tomorrow. When I arrive back on the 9th floor I go into the office with a smile on my face. I walk past Angel and she looks at me with a look of curiosity. I know she's dying to know why I'm grinning. I feel good. I feel alive. *Damn, all that just from a ten-dollar meal and some male attention.* I hope I still feel this good after my talk with Gina tonight.

Joan:

That girl is something else! I had a lot on my mind and really just needed some girl time. She had to ruin it with propositioning me. Now I have even more on my mind. I thought we were friends, but she was treating me like I was just a prostitute. It's not so much the act that I'm messed up about. I've had sex with women, while I was dressed as a woman. When you are a sex worker and you're about that paper, there isn't much that you won't do. The only thing I won't do is perform in the presence of a child.

One man wanted me to perform sexual paid favors while his kid was asleep in the back seat. That's some sick shit. You got that much of a problem that you can't wait until your kid's not around. I almost gave this man some serious head, but when I leaned down to unzip the monster that was trying to get out of his pants, I heard something in the back seat. I was so shocked to see a little girl-she had to be about three years old. Thank God, she stirred in her sleep. I would have never forgiven myself for traumatizing a child. She could have woken up and seen my mouth wrapped around her daddy's dick. Who knows what type of problems that would have created for her later in life. I cussed his ass out and took his money. I threatened to tell the police about this incident if he didn't get the fuck out of here. I took a picture with my phone of his daughter. I already had a picture of his license plate. I always did that before getting into anyone's car. He had the choice to leave without his money or risk the police questioning him at his home.

He chose to give me my money and drive off not wanting to risk any potential future drama. That night I met Karma; which was the same night that I had to go to the hospital. Well, this dude is the reason why I had to go to the hospital. He set me up. He came back later that day

alone. When I say alone, I mean with no kids in the back. He apologized to me and asked if he

could get some head. He showed me the money and I got in. I double checked that nobody was

in the back seat. He pulled over towards a dead-end street and ordered me to go to work. I did

what I was paid to do. As soon as he came in my mouth, the passenger side car door opened.

Somebody punched me in my head just as I sat up to swallow. I choked a little on the semen.

 I was stunned for about five long seconds. The punch was so powerful my head ended up

back on the tricks lap. As my head lay on his lap, he zips his pants up aggressively and a piece of

my lip gets cut by the zipper. I try to raise my head again. I'm still a little dazed. I look him in

the eye and spit whatever I had left in my mouth in his face. *Sick motherfucker.*

I remember thinking that I was going to fuck him up. He was obviously letting the dress

fool him. As soon as the thought entered my head to whoop the both of their asses, I feel myself

being shocked. *They tased me.* The two of them started to pummel me. Most of their blows

landed on my torso. I couldn't fight back.

At the point where I could no longer feel the pain from the blows, they pushed me out of

the car and took off. I was hurt. I was numb. In an alley traveled more by rats than by actual

people, I was left to fend for myself.. Nobody walking on the main street noticed that I was down

there. I didn't yell for help. I thought that I was going to die. Many times, I've toyed with idea of

ending my life. That night, I wasn't sure if I wanted to live. I just laid there.

I must have passed out. When I woke up, I remembered dreaming about my mother. She

kept telling me to fight. "Fight Joan, Fight!" I love my mother. She didn't call me Jonathan. If

she wanted Joan to fight, that's what Joan was going to do. With the little strength that I had, I

82

got myself up. I didn't have to walk far. Once I made it out of the alley, I saw a woman in the parking lot across the street get into her car. She just sat there. She didn't drive off. I paused. I wanted to see if she was waiting on someone. After a few minutes went by, I approached her vehicle hoping that she'd have some compassion. Thank God for Karma.

Eve:

I arrive to a spotless apartment. Gina took cleaning to another level when she was sober. When she's high, our home would look like a homeless shelter. She didn't care. I look at the walls. I know she didn't give the place a paint job so she must've wipe down the walls a few times. It seemed brighter in here. I guess Gina didn't feel like cooking and cleaning. A large box of pizza is sitting on the kitchen table. All that's missing is the pink lemonade. As quickly as that thought popped into my mind, Gina opens the refrigerator door and pulls out two glasses of pink lemonade with a healthy amount of ice in it. She already had our glasses chilling in the refrigerator. I don't know who this Gina is, but I could get used to her.

"Hey Gina. It looks good in here. What--did you do hire a maid service?"

"Girl you know I wouldn't bring no strangers into your place."

"I know Gina. I'm just messing with you. Thanks for cleaning this place up."

"No problem. It's the least I can do."

"Let's eat this pizza before it gets cold. Pass me one of those glasses of lemonade."

Neither one of us say anything while we are eating. I can tell that Gina is nervous. I must have her feeling like I'm the mother and she's the child that has to explain herself. Well, serves her right. My childhood was a living hell. She didn't do a good job raising me, nurturing me or providing for me. I had to fend for myself. Now, it's time for her to explain herself. I already know that she's not my biological mom. What I want to know is who Gina is and why she agreed to keep me. Gina picks up her glass of pink lemonade. Takes a sip. Sighs and then begins.

"First of all, I never agreed to raise you. My cousin came down to Charlotte from Dorchester to visit me. I hadn't seen her in years, but we kept in touch over the phone. She called me the week before saying that she had something to tell me, but she wanted to wait until we were face-to-face. I couldn't imagine what she had to tell me and why it needed to be told in person.

When she arrives, she arrives with you. I'm thinking that she up and had a baby and didn't tell me. I assume that this is what she had to tell me. My cousin was only here for a weekend before she up and left. You see, my shady cousin, sold drugs and pussy for this dude named Craig from Boston. I'd never met him, but I heard some stories about him. He was her pimp. She said that she got pregnant by him, but didn't tell him that the baby was his. She lied and said it was some tricks. At least that is what she told me.

My no-good cousin asked if she could stay with me for a while until she figured out her next move. She was trying to get away from Craig. Of course, I told her she could stay. I had two bedrooms. She was welcomed to stay in the spare one. I woke up Sunday morning to you crying and my cousin nowhere to be found. She left a note saying *"This baby is just going to slow me down. Whatever you do, don't let Craig have her."* And that was it. I only saw her one more time after that. It was when you were ten. Remember that time you came home from school and I was fighting with that lady? She was wearing a hot pink mini skirt and long blonde wig. Well that was her. She wanted you back after leaving you with me for ten years.

She abandoned you. I wouldn't let her have you. I knew why she wanted you. She wanted to sell you to the highest bidder. I may have been getting high back then, but I wasn't that high. I wasn't giving you back to her. You were mine. I threatened to beat her ass if she ever came sniffing around here again. I also threatened to contact Craig. I told her to imagine what he would do to her after finding out she kept his kid from him for ten years.

She left and never came back. I felt bad for you, that's why I kept you. I was too young to have a child. My lifestyle didn't have any room for a child. I was selling drugs. I could afford to raise you. I just didn't know how to. She left you with her drug dealing cousin that had an addiction problem. You had no business with me, but that alternative was far worse.

I regret that I exposed you to all the bad shit that was going on in my life. I tried my best with you. I know that I wasn't a good mother to you. I knew that I wouldn't be good mother in general. So, I made sure that I wouldn't fuck any other kid's life up and I had my tubes tied. I didn't trust myself to stop using. I've been using drugs since I was a teenager; using was in my bloodline.

I was told that I was addicted when I was born. My maternal grandmother raised me, but she was also my foster mother. The state got custody of me before I was able to leave the hospital. They placed me with my mother's mother. Although she got paid to take care of me, I know she loved me. I was a sick baby and she nurtured me back to health. Life was good. I have nothing but good memories of my grandmother.

My mom was allowed to have supervised visits with me at my grandmother's home. I saw her every once and a while. She would come to the house to eat or borrow money. My grandmother never would give her any money; that's probably why she robbed her. I'll never forget that day. I came home from my afterschool program and found the police at our home.

The police weren't alone. My social worker was there too. It was a Wednesday. The next time I saw my grandmother was a week later at her funeral. The robbery went bad. My grandmother had a heart attack during the robbery. After that, I was placed in foster care with one shady family after another. I couldn't tell you how many homes that I ran away from. The social worker couldn't stand me. She always had a hard time placing me. I was labeled as a "runner". I also became a "cutter", but that's another story. I knew I could sign myself out of state custody, when I turned eighteen. That's what I did. By that time, I was already using drugs and involved with the wrong people. Five years later, my cousin calls me and I get you."

"So, why didn't you put me in foster care if you knew you wouldn't do a good job raising me? Why keep me and raise me as if I'm some science project?"

"I'd never put you into foster care. I know what happens in foster care. I didn't want to risk you getting touched by some pervert. Perverts aren't just men nowadays. Some of the women are nasty too."

"Well, Gina, I guess I should appreciate the fact that you thought about me enough not to put me in to foster care with the perverts." I say this with a ton of sarcasm. By the look on Gina's face, I know that what I say next will stun her. I'm coming in strong from the left field.

"Instead, you found a live-in pervert for us. You let Mr. Uncle have his way with me. You knew! Don't even act as if this is a surprise. You knew that he was sticking his old dick inside of me. You couldn't possible think he was that into you. Your ass was always high. While you sucked a pipe, I was sucking dick!"

Gina has tears in her eyes. I realize that I do too once the tears involuntarily drop. We are both crying. I'm not really crying. Tears are falling, but I'm not filled with emotion. She clearly is. Snot is running down her lips. She looks pitiful, but she'll get no pity from me. She makes no effort to wipe the snot away. I make no effort to go get her a tissue. We just look at each other. She knew or she wouldn't have been crying. I don't feel sorry for her. She should feel sorry for me. *That bitch knew.*

I'm upset. I imagined I'd be enraged; so being only upset is a plus. I thought that I'd want to cause some serious bodily harm to Gina for all the neglect and abuse she exposed me to. Instead, I feel nothing. We both just sit and look at each other. A few minutes go by without either of us speaking. We just sit there letting the shame run through us. Finally, she says something that doesn't make it all better, but it slightly cracked open the door for forgiveness.

"You saved my life. Every time I quit using, you were the reason. Every time I got myself together and got a job, you were the reason. I owe you my life. I had so many reasons to take one hit too many and end my life. You kept me from overdosing. You had nobody but me. I had to stay alive for you. In the end, I'm the only one that benefited from our relationship. I'm sorry that I used you and didn't protect you. Despite your dysfunctional upbringing, you are an exceptional woman. I admire your resilience. I admire your strength. You never turned to drugs. You didn't repeat my vicious cycle. You survived. I wish I were more like you."

Again, we sit in silence. I don't respond immediately. I need to process what she just said. I need to let it marinate. In my head, I say *Fuck you! Karma's a bitch and I can't wait for you to meet her.* What comes out of my mouth is "Let's find healing together."

Claudia:

Rochelle comes by without calling first. I'm guessing that Ava's daddy told her what I said. She has balls--I'll give her that. I let her in without saying anything to her. I let her get uncomfortable with the silence. Most people can't handle silence for too long, especially people like Rochelle. She broke the silence.

"You can't be mad that I was still fucking Ava's father" Rochelle blurts out.

"Bitch, you are just a trifling ass hoe. I shouldn't be surprised." I say disgustedly.

"Whatever Claudia. You're just in your feelings as usual. What more do you want from me? I gave you my kid. Your old ass been living a lie for fifty years and now you got yourself believing it."

"Oh, you gave me your kid huh? Is that how it went? I asked you for your kid and you just gave her to me. No bitch. That's not what happened. My memory may be a little shaky these days, but I didn't forget how shit went down. You went behind my back and fucked my man. We both got pregnant at the same time, by the same man. You begged me to take care of your child. The child that you never wanted." I feel myself instinctively rolling my neck at Rochelle.

"The way I remember it is that you lost your baby and hated the fact that you weren't going to get a chance to use the baby to trap that white boy. Yes, I fucked your man and got pregnant by him. I thought we were past that. You lost your baby a day after you delivered her. I felt bad for you. Here we were both having a baby for the same man. You loved him and I was just drunk and horny. Neither one of us believe in killing babies, but you and I both knew that I didn't want a child. So, it was ideal for both of us. Don't make it seem like it was just ideal for me.

I cried for you Claudia. I can't imagine what it feels like to carry a child, deliver it and then wake up the next morning to find out your child didn't make it through the night. That same morning, my child is being born. I asked you to raise the child of the man that you loved. The man that you delivered a child for. I know you thought he'd leave his wife for you but he didn't. What neither of us planned on was him not stepping up to the plate to raise Ava.

Throughout all of these years, I never told anyone. I told folks that I lost the baby. I will admit; I got the sympathy that you should've gotten, but you got a child. You got Ava. You and I have a similar build and she ended up looking just like her daddy. Nobody ever thought to question it. And now fifty years later, after our daughter Ava is dead and gone, you want to throw shade."

"What the fuck do you mean our daughter is *dead and gone*?"

Karma:

Joan's been giving me the cold shoulder. She's still mad at me for last time that we chilled together. I texted her a few times inviting her out and she declined every time. I'm the last person to sweat a bitch. *Fuck it.* She'll come around. I decide that I am going to pay Eve a surprise visit. Gina answered Eve's phone last week when I called. Eve was in the shower and Karma had me saved in her phone as "bestie". I guess Gina thought it was ok to take the call or she was just nosey. Either way, I told her that I wanted to surprise Eve. I asked for her address and to make sure that she didn't tell her that we spoke. Gina promised that she wouldn't.

Today, I am in Richard's home catching up. He offered to let me stay there while I'm in town, but I tell him that wouldn't be smart. He is telling me this crazy ass story about someone breaking into his home and destroying his plumbing. The person had to be crazy as hell. They left urine and feces on top of a cemented toilet bowl. "Who does that?" he says to me.

Guys are so clueless. How could he not know who did this? I already know it's some female that he fucked. She's obviously bitter. I guess she felt shitted on and wanted him to feel the same way. I'll give it to her; she definitely left her mark. He'll never forget that day.

Richard is kissing me on my neck just the way that I like. Lord knows that I am ready to get the party started, but I need to get to Eve's place at a specific time. I can't get caught up in Richard's lustful web and miss my opportunity to surprise her. I tell Richard that I'll see him later tonight and that he can come by the Marriott and pick up where we left off.

Eve lives about thirty minutes away from Richard so it doesn't take me to long. Gina opens the door for me when I arrive. She looks nothing like I imagined. I guess I thought she'd

90

look like a strung-out crack head; She's a very good looking woman. Gina has deep brown skin. She is wearing an auburn page-boy wig. I can't tell what her natural hair looks like. She looks like she's a size ten. I thought she'd be skinny. Her eyes have a slant to them. It makes me thing that she has some Asian ancestry. The cubic zirconia stud in her nose looks like it has seen better days. It has lost its luster. Her clothes are cheap, but you can tell she went out of her way to look nice for me. I guess she wanted to look good for Eve's friend from Boston. She has no idea that I'm really her sister.

I have take-out from the soul food restaurant Nana's. I remember Eve mentioning that she enjoys their Macaroni and cheese with candied yams. So, I bought that with some fried chicken and greens. I wasn't sure what Gina liked, but figured everyone likes fried chicken. I got enough for a family of five so they'd have left-overs for at least two days. Gina sets the dinette set.

"Damn Gina! What you cooking up in here. It smells g...! Eve stops dead in her tracks when she sees me in her kitchen. She actually drops her bottle of water that she has in her hand.

"Hey Sis! Surprise!" I yell in an excited voice tone.

"Karma What are you doing here? How'd you know where I live?"

She's clearly not happy to see me. She's definitely surprised, but she's not happy. I don't like the vibe that she is giving off. I'm ready to check her, but her mother is witnessing this.

"I wanted it to be a surprise!" I use my fake customer service voice tone. I walk over to her and give her a hug. She hugs me back, but I can feel it's not genuine. It feels like she's afraid of me or something. I don't know what's up, but we will get to the bottom of it tonight. I'm not leaving Charlotte without finding out what her fucking problem is. She obviously got

91

everything worked out with Gina. It looks like she is living here. So, what the fuck is her problem?

We all eat and shoot the shit. Gina is filling me in on everything I've missed while Eve is eating everything in sight. She's not saying much. Surprisingly, I'm hitting it off with Gina. I can't speak on how she was back when she was raising Eve, but she seems like good people now that she is sober.

Gina excuses herself so that Eve and I could catch up. Eve is hiding something. I want to know what. Then I remember. I never told her that I sent her that text. I was just fucking with her; I would never rat her out. I guess I didn't think too much about it. I figured it would've fucked with her that day, but not this long. She never reached out to me about it. And I never felt the need to let her know it was me that texted her. But why didn't she reach out to me? We were sisters. We did some things together that could get us both locked up. We both had dirt on each other. I didn't kill anyone, but I'm not one to judge one sin over another.

When Gina is out of earshot I address the fat ass elephant in the room.

"What the fuck is your problem bitch? I fly out her to see your ass and you treat me like I'm a fucking bill collector. Let's just get this shit right out in the open. Is there some shit that you want to talk to me about? Is there some shit that I did to you that you are holding against me? If so, let me know right now. Let's clear this up bitch!"

"I've got a lot on my mind Karma. It has nothing to do with you and it's nothing you can help me with. I have to handle this myself. I just didn't expect you to show up at my door. It's not like I invited you. I didn't give anyone my address because I wanted to work through some things in my life. My plan was to come back to Boston and continue with life where I left it."

"So, you were going to come back to Boston after you worked through your issues with Gina or after things die down with Cynthia's murder investigation? I know you knew that there was a camera in the room. You were careful not to show your face. You were also in disguise, but *I know you*. I know your stride. I know your mannerisms. You didn't fool me. That's why I sent you that text. I was mad that you didn't confide in me. Did you think that I would tell the police or better yet Craig? Is that why you were avoiding me? I really thought we had a bond. Shit. We are sisters--at least I thought we were. I got you Eve. You could have come to me. You didn't have to kill her. That shit was fucked up. We could've gotten back at Uncle Craig without killing anyone. You should've known that I had your back."

"I was soooooo angry Karma. I just needed him to feel pain and loss the way that I did."

"Ok, I get it. You were mad because you didn't get the chance to know your mother, but here's what you aren't considering. You are still here! And it's because *he* didn't kill *you*. He let you live. Craig is a ruthless motherfucker. He showed compassion by letting you live. The person to blame for this madness is Ben. He treated both of our mothers like shit. He was fucking my mother while he was with your mother. He raped and disfigured my mother. My mother should've had Ben killed, but she didn't because she wanted me to have a father in my life. Is my life better because I had access to my father? What's the good in having a living, breathing father and he be an awful role model? He was there for me financially, but he really wasn't around. My mom was my mother and father."

"At least your mother raised you." Eve says sounding like a victim.

I can't stand a person that throws their self a pity party and expects you to join.

"Look bitch. You had a mother. Gina was your mother. Charlene gave birth to you, but Gina raised you. You may have had a shitty beginning, but you are in control of your present and future. You over here mourning a ghost you never knew. Fix the relationship that you have with your real mother. She's right in the other room, not buried six feet deep." I feel a tinge of guilt for saying it, but she needs to get it together.

Gina walks into the room. She was eavesdropping. I guess she learned a few things by listening in. She sits down beside Eve. We both tell her everything that we know.

"Ain't this some shit. You ain't my cousin's baby? That hoe was hired to kidnap you. I knew my cousin could be trifling; this takes it to another level." Gina shakes her head and then goes to the refrigerator to refill her lemonade. She sits back down. "So y'all two are sisters."

Eve phone rings. It's on the table next to the candied yams. We can all see the name that pops up. It says GREG. She smiles. I guess she has new dick in her life.

It All Makes Sense

Claudia:

How the fuck don't I remember my own daughter's funeral? Karma must think I'm crazy. I showed up to the house asking her where her mother was and when she was coming back. Poor thing. I must really be worse off than I thought. Something is definitely wrong with me.

After Rochelle and I cuss each other out, we squash our beef. She fills me in on the funeral that I don't remember being in attendance of. I cry. I don't cry. I wail. I'm horrified that I didn't know Ava died. Well, I did know, but I didn't remember. It's time for me to admit to the things I've been experiencing. I need help. I still want to keep as much independence as possible but I know what I have to do. I ask Rochelle to move in with me to help me and she accepts. I'm losing time. I need her to be here to keep time for me.

Rochelle made me write an affidavit stating that she is living here, free of charge. We get it notarized while I'm still in my right mind. The last thing that she needs is to be arrested at this age for being an intruder because my dementia having ass couldn't remember her. She can live here until the day that she dies for all I care. She suggested that I tell Karma. I told her that I would at some point, but not yet.

She moves her stuff in and makes herself right at home. I make sure to tell her that I don't want a bunch of people that I don't know up in here. I ask that she keep her visitors to a minimum. Her smart-ass replies "You won't remember either way." We both can't help but laugh. I am grateful to have her help because she's someone that won't baby me. She'll treat me the same. That's exactly what I need. The last thing that I want is for someone to be in here trying to help me while treating me like a toddler.

I make plans to invite Karma over for dinner. I need to tell her about my condition. I also need to get to a doctor to learn more about what I can expect. If there are any drugs I can take to slow down the progression, I want them. This has become priority so I make an appointment with my primary care physician. One thing I'm not going to do is feel sorry for myself. I'm not about that pity party life. I taught Ava not to be that way and I know that she taught Karma not to be that way either. We may have a lot of issues in our family, but we are some strong women.

After I make my doctor's appointment, I call Karma to invite her over for dinner this Sunday. We need to talk. Instead of calling, she texts me back. She says that she's in Charlotte and won't be back in time. Concerned, she asks if everything is ok and I assure her that I'm fine. She let me know that she'll be back in two weeks. We can have dinner then.

Two weeks should be enough time to get my things in order. Who knows when this disease is going to take over. I need to do everything while I'm still in my right mind. I make plans to meet with an attorney and get my assets in order. She doesn't know it, but I plan on leaving some money to Rochelle. I'm not going to tell her. She relied on the support of men her entire life so she never had any real money. Now she will. It's time she didn't have to rely on men. Besides, her coochie got to be tired by now.

Joan:

I went by Karma's condo, but she wasn't there. I went by her family home and she wasn't there either. Well, I don't know if she was there or not. Her cars were at the family home but nobody answered the door. I didn't call her because I didn't want to talk to her over the phone. I wanted to talk to her face-to-face. I wanted to tell her that she's risking our friendship by having me sleep with her for payment towards my operation.

I don't want her money. Now, don't get me wrong, I've wanted this surgery for a very long time. I'm not above doing something strange for some change. This surgery isn't on my want list--it's on my need list. I need it for my sanity. The problem is that I value the friendship that Karma and I are building. I don't want to risk it. There has to be another way that I can get her to help me without compromising our friendship. Maybe she could loan me the money. I could pay her off each month. I know that she's addicted to sex but I don't know if she knows she is. Some therapy would help. We all have our issues, but I don't want her to choose her addiction over our friendship. I believe that she came into my life for a reason.

***

On a whim, I applied for a job at the MAC counter at Macy's in the Cambridge Side Galleria Mall. I didn't think that they'd hire me, but they did. Today is my first day so now I have two jobs; if I count my after-hours job. My night job pays good money. It gives me enough to pay my bills and eat. I really have to work for that money though. My apartment isn't subsidized so I have to pay a lot of money to live in Cambridge.

After I graduated from high school, I didn't know what I wanted to do with myself. My mom was disappointed because I didn't want to go to college. High school was difficult for me. Each year I transitioned a little more. If you didn't know me as Jonathan, you'd have a hard time finding any traces of him judging by my appearance.

It's no lie, kids can be cruel. I got called all types of names. The one that I hated the most was "Shim". That was a combination between the word "she" and "him". Each year was more dreadful than the year before. High school was more like torture than anything else. When I finally stopped going to the men's bathroom and started going to the women's bathroom, some folks had a problem with it. I remember days when I'd go the entire day without going to the bathroom. I held it because the Principal warned that me utilizing the women's bathroom would have severe consequences.

I have more than a few bad memories of high school. One in particular stood out. It was the morning my home-room teacher--the one that looked like she struggled with her sexuality--asked me to go to the Principal's office. I just arrived at school. I couldn't think of anything that I did to warrant a visit to the Principal's office. Nonetheless, I did as I was told. As I walked through the corridor, I racked my brain. All I did today was go to the bathroom. Then I went to the cafeteria to get some breakfast. After that I went to homeroom and was asked to go see the Principal.

"The Principal will see you now." The lady at the front desk didn't even give me eye contact. I walk into the Principal's office and sit down in the chair directly in front of his desk.

"Jonathan, do you know why you have been called to my office?"

I cringe when he calls me Jonathan.

"No Principal Douglass, I don't."

"Jonathan, just because you've been dressing up as a woman doesn't mean you are one."

"Why are you saying this to me? And by the way, I prefer that I'm called Joan."

"You can prefer Joan all you want. Your transcript and your birth certificate say Jonathan. As a matter of fact, I'm glad you brought that up. There's no mystery surrounding what I have to say and why you're getting detention. You cannot use the girls' bathroom. You are not a woman. You are a man. If I come to school tomorrow with a dress and high heels on and tell you to call me Sherry; that doesn't make me a woman.

If I catch you using the girls' bathroom again, I'm going to report you to the authorities. I'll let them know you've been disciplined for frequenting the girls' bathroom. Some girls have complained that they don't feel safe and rightfully so. You know what comes next Jonathan?" You'll be on your way to being tagged as a sex offender. Do you want to be looked at as a sex offender? I think not. So, let this be the last time that I hear that you were in the girl's bathroom. You have detention for an hour after class today. I'm tired of all you boys playing dress up in my school! You're dismissed."

"Principal Douglass…the bathroom says boys and girls. It doesn't say penises and vaginas. Maybe you should change the signs to make it a little bit more clear for your transgender population that your ignorant behind thinks is playing dress up!"

My last comment got me a week's worth of detention. That happened in eleventh grade. By twelfth grade, I had too many visits to the urologist. I'd hold my pee throughout the entire school day. I wouldn't go to the bathroom. I didn't feel comfortable going to the men's bathroom and the girls didn't feel comfortable with me using their bathroom. High School sucked. It's a miracle that I learned anything, because I was stressed out every day. I wasn't ready to take a chance with college.

Instead, I went to hair school. I got hired by Michael Rawston Jr.; one of the best hair stylist in New England. He visited my hair school back when I was a student. The instructor told me that Michael Rawston Jr. was impressed with my work. Once I heard that, I'll admit, my head got a little big for the day. As luck or skill would have it, he offered me a job a month before graduation. I didn't even have to apply.

I stopped doing hair at J. Michael Salon when he closed up shop. It wasn't that the business was failing. The business was doing well. It was doing so well that a celebrity asked Michael to be their personal stylist. I forget who it was. They offered him so much money that he couldn't turn it down. He made sure that all of his stylist had a place to work before closing up shop. He really had a conscience. Michael cared about us. He wanted to see all his stylist excel and be successful. I'm the only one that didn't go to work for another salon.

I love doing hair and make-up, but I loved doing it at J. Michael Salon. I didn't want to try to start over at a new salon. Then I'd have to get them used to me; a transgender woman. So instead, I started waitressing. I soon found out that waitressing didn't bring in enough money. My rent was expensive. I needed more money. One of the assistant managers at the restaurant I was working at put me on to her side hustle. Prostitution.

After my first weekend of testing the after-hours waters; I stopped waitressing and started tricking full-time. There was a whole underworld of people that wanted to have sex with trans women. They paid good money too. It was easier than waitressing. The men that wanted to have sex with me made me feel beautiful. They made me feel good about myself. The men knew what I was and still desired me. They treated me like the woman that I am.

When my mom found out what I was doing, she was disappointed. She said that she was afraid for my safety. I assured her that I was safe and took precautions. I needed to do this until I figured out what I wanted to do with my life. She offered to pay my rent until I figured out what I wanted to do. She was so sweet. I turned her down though. She shouldn't have to pay for my indecisiveness. I wouldn't let her. I told her that I wouldn't do it for long and that I'd eventually go back to doing hair and make-up.

After two years of asking when I would go back to doing hair and make-up, she finally stopped asking. And I'm finally back at it. I'll see how things go at MAC. It's not going to pay me enough to survive without my night job, but at least I won't have to work at night as much. That's progress. I know that my mom would be happy about that.

My mother and I used to have candid conversations about what I was experiencing and what I could expect to experience. She loved to research things. Instead of being ashamed of me--like I thought she'd be-- she researched what was going on with me. In fact, she's the person that hipped me to GID. I didn't even know my issues had a name.

"Gender Identity Disorder is the distress that you feel as a result of the sex or gender God gave you at birth. It's an actual diagnosis Joan. GID is classified as a disorder; they call it Gender Dysphoria. Joan, I've seen you battle depression most of your teenage years. You acted confident, but I knew that you had a low self-esteem. You'd isolate yourself. You worried me. Everyone knows that I am not big on meds. Why choose meds for things God can fix? But I saw myself losing you. I didn't want to walk into your bedroom and find that you took the fast track to be with the Lord. So, I put my beliefs on the back burner and allowed the doctors to prescribe you anxiety meds.

That's why I am also going to allow you to go on hormones. I'm smart enough to know that this isn't some kind of rebellious act. I know that you are suffering. And if we are going to go through this, we have to be smart about it. We are going to make sure that you are diagnosed with suffering from GID. That way, if you decide to have sexual reassignment therapy or surgery, our health insurance will cover it. If you don't get the diagnosis, they will classify it as a cosmetic procedure and wont' cover you."

"Damn Mom, you really did your research. I'm not surprised though. I'm really blessed to have you as a mother. Knowing that I have your support no matter what has made me stronger." I tell her this while I hug her tightly. I'll never forget what she said next.

"Joan, I can't imagine being disgusted by dick."

Did she just say that? "Mom, you only know what dick feels like in you, not attached to you. Believe me, it's very different."

"I guess so!" she said cracking up.

Those are the types of conversations I was able to have with my mom when she was living. She's always had my back. I don't know why I was ever afraid to reveal my true self to her. Unfortunately, I can't say that the rest of the family was as supportive and open-minded as my Mom. A Thanksgiving Dinner, I'll never forget, revealed that to me. I was fourteen years old.

We'd all head over to my grandmother's house for dinner. It was like a huge family reunion. There were thirty of us at my grandmother's. Surprisingly, we were all able to fit comfortably. Thank God she had an open floor plan. She had three dining room tables connected in the shape of a horse shoe. That set up allowed everyone to be able engage with each other. I

103

remember wishing that I was sitting at one of the ends of the table; not at the base, like I was, which was directly in the middle. Sitting there, I felt like all eyes were on me. It was during the beginning stages of me transitioning. I didn't want any questions directed at me so I tried to look as normal as possible for the sake of saving face.

My grandmother was something else when she had a few too many. Everyone was fair game. She'd tell you about yourself with no filter. Luckily for me, but unfortunately for my older cousin Gary Jr, Grandma took it upon herself to target Cousin Gary this Thanksgiving.

At that time, Cousin Gary hadn't come out of the closet, but it was obvious that he is gay. Most of the family smiled in his face, but talked about him when he was out of earshot. Everyone, except my mom and his parents acted like he was the black sheep. The family treated him like shit. If I was him, I would have stopped coming to Thanksgiving dinner at Grandma's house.

"Gary, do you really have to bring that madness to our family dinner each year? Couldn't you be a little more masculine for one day. Then you can go back to acting gay once you get home. It makes me sick that you sashay around here like you're a woman. Toughen up Boy! This family ain't got no room for sissies. Thank God, your grandfather is dead and gone. He'd be disgraced."

Nobody said anything. Grandma wasn't even drunk yet. The room was eerily quiet after my grandmother spoke. Out of nowhere, my mother says "Mama, you need to treat Gary better. You are a woman of God. You go to church every Sunday. What good is it to know the bible inside and out if you act like you never read a page. Gary isn't choosing to be gay. Being gay isn't a choice. All y'all at this table act like you don't have any battles. Y'all act like we don't

104

have any family secrets. You better stop treating family like criminals before certain family members get fed up and open the flood gates letting all the family skeletons float out." After that, nobody said anything. I stopped going to Thanksgiving dinner at Grandma's house a few years after that. I got tired of faking the funk. And, I didn't want to be judged the way that Gary was. So instead of going to grandma's, Mom started having folks over to her house for Thanksgiving dinner.

BJ:

She thinks she's slick. She's just a user. I thought we were friends, but I obviously thought wrong. Karma just keeps me around in case she needs something. I know this and I still stick around. All she does is use people. Yet, she takes using to another level with this motivational speaking hustle.

I set Karma up with ten couples that want to spice up their love lives. This is her first group to test her motivational speaking skills. We are at the Marriott in one of their meeting rooms. Folks haven't started to arrive. I'm nervous. Karma is confident. I ask her if she wants to practice on me, but she says no. Five minutes later, couples begin entering the room. Once every seat is filled. Karma begins.

She does a tremendous job. She's a natural. *Why am I surprised?* After all, she did convince me to do some things I thought that I never would. I am so proud of her. She has them eating out of the palm of her hand. They are hanging on to every seductive word. However, what throws me for a loop is what she says next. She closes by saying that she is available for individual couple sessions. I think she's lost her mind. She failed to inform me that she'd be making house calls. What's worse is she actually says that she'll come to their homes and tutor them. The first fifteen minutes will be no charge, if they signed up for her next speaking engagement. If she stays longer than that, she charges $100 every fifteen minutes.

That sounds like prostitution to me. I silently pray that folks pick up on it and won't bite. But my prayer fails. Every single couple signs up for her to come to their home. Karma is promising to heighten their pleasure dramatically. She has them hooked. She even had the audacity to ask me to come along. Initially, I declined; but somehow, she talked me into just being there as a "chaperone." She'd pay me $100 for each appointment she'd make. As usual, Karma got her way.

We arrive at the first couple's home. It is a rainy, Sunday afternoon. The couple is just getting home from church. They still have their Bibles in their hands when Karma and I arrive. Karma sits down with the couple and instructs them to get undressed and to put on the robe that she purchased for them. I wonder what she has in her big ole' bag.

They both do as they are told and meet Karma and I in their bedroom. The couple looks to be in their mid-forties. They are an inter-racial couple - the husband is white and the wife is Asian. The husband is in great shape. I mean he is built like a super hero. The wife definitely had some work done. She's a size zero with a D cup.

Karma doesn't allow me to sit in on the actual fifteen-minute motivational counseling session. She wants to keep the couple's issues as private as possible. She tells me that she wants to gain their trust and she can't do it with me in the room. If their session goes over fifteen minutes, that's when my job comes in.

My job is to observe and take notes. I suggest that we film it, but Karma insists on no cameras. She also requires that they have enough cash for an hour session placed on the table. She explains to the couple that she doesn't want to interrupt any moments to collect payment. At the hour mark, everything will stop and they will assess if additional time is needed. If so, cash will be required at that time up front.

Fifteen minutes is up. Karma comes out of their bedroom and tells me to get my notepad. She tells me that I am not permitted to talk or ask questions while in the session. I need to be invisible. I am to take notes on the interaction between the couple. At first, I'm confused. *Was I supposed to just write down what was going on in the room?* Seeing the confusion on my face, she clarifies what she means. She tells me that I'm to write down what the couple responds to physically. If the husband sucks on his wife's left nipple and she enjoys it, write it down. If the husband sucks on his wife's left nipple and she's unresponsive, write it down. It's as simple as that. I'm to write down what each person responds to. Sounds easy enough.

I enter the room and everyone is naked--including Karma. The robes that she gave them were on the floor. I'm shocked and instantly turned on by Karma's naked body. This may be harder than I thought. *Why is this bitch naked?* Karma points to a chair that's positioned in the corner. All eyes are on me. I slowly sit down and place my note pad on my lap. The pen is placed behind my right ear. I remove it and place it between my index and middle finger as if I'm holding a cigarette.

The lights are dim. A song starts to play. It's an old-school R&B song by Faith Evans. I only recognize it because I'm a fan of 90's music. The song is slow and seductive. The couple was previously told that only sounds could be made, no words. There will be no words spoken by or to anyone during this session. Karma is the only one allowed to speak.

Everyone, except me, is naked. The white guy's dick is already erect. I imagine it's because he has two naked women in his bedroom. All three of them are on a king size bed. The couple is sitting up next to each other, with their backs resting on the massive cherry wood head board. Neither one of them are touching. Karma is standing at the foot of the bed facing them. Faith Evans' voice is serenading the room. The lyrics *"Soon as I get home, I'll make it up to you, Baby I'll do what I gotta do"* are heard. Karma walks over to the right side of the bed and licks the Asian woman's left nipple. I didn't know that Karma was going to be the one doing the nipple licking when she told me what I'd be doing.

I'm watching Karma lick this woman's nipples and I secretly wish it is me that she is tasting. As I'm watching Karma, Karma is watching me. I realize that she is looking at me because I'm not writing. *Who can write under these circumstances*? I start writing. Karma then proceeds to show both nipples some serious attention. I notice the husband's dick jump. He's mesmerized at what he's witnessing. The wife is moaning.

The woman is no longer leaning against her headboard. She is now laying down on her back. Karma places her hand over the woman's mouth. She covers her mouth so that she can't yell. She then expertly glides a dildo inside of her. I can see the woman gasp although her mouth is covered. Karma has obviously done this before. It's hard to write. It's hard to do anything but watch. The husband looks like he's in a trance. He starts to stroke himself, but Karma orders him to stop. He doesn't listen. Karma continues to seduce his wife. She's licking all over this woman's body. The husband is in ecstasy. I'm turned on and angry at the same time. It's hard

not to be aroused when watching other people being pleasured. The wife's moans are making me

wet.

Why would Karma pick me to watch this shit? She knows how I feel about her. She

knows that I love her. She knows that this will make me jealous. She really has no conscience.

This will be my first and last time working with Karma. I watch and listen as Karma puts the

wife's hand on the dildo and tells her to take over. She then scoots over to the woman's husband.

What the hell is she about to do? She sits on his unprotected pink dick and rides him

backwards. Her titties are bouncing up and down. I just want to put my mouth on them. I

remember what they feel like against my tongue. I think about other places my tongue has

explored on her body. She guides this man's hands to her tits and locks in eye contact with me.

She addresses the wife, but is staring at me. Her voice tone changes. It now has authority.

"Mmmmmm. Watch me ride your husband's thick dick! Watch him give it to me the way

he's gonna give it to you! Show him with that dildo how you're gonna take all of his dick. Show

him!"

The husband is fucking the shit out of Karma. The wife is slamming the dildo up inside

of her like she is accustomed to rough sex. The husband and wife are looking at each other get

pleased by someone and something other than them. Karma then demands that they better come

when she says so. She counts to ten and then orders them to come. All four of us climax

simultaneously. Karma gets up and semen is dripping from her coochie. I'm grossed out. I'm

disgusted. She doesn't even know this man. She just fucked him raw. Something is seriously

wrong with Karma. Something is seriously wrong with me for loving her.

I allow my heartbeat to settle down for a minute. I'm embarrassed. I stand up and walk out without saying a word. Karma watches me leave. She doesn't say anything to stop me; she just stares. She knows that I am leaving. I'm not sure if she knows that I am leaving for good. She doesn't respect herself enough for my taste. Does she think she's immune to HIV?

I place the notebook down on the night stand. I want to throw it on the bed and hope it lands on all of their bodily fluids. Karma is a sick bitch. I don't know what kind of sessions she thinks she's running but it looks and smells like prostitution. What I do know is that I am not the one! I won't be going to jail for the shit she's doing. I love my freedom more than I love Karma. Exiting the couple's home, I tell myself to remember this feeling. Hopefully, I'll remember it the next time Karma tries to contact me and avoid her.

Craig:

Folks underestimate me. Never underestimate a man on a mission. I have a plan in place to find out who killed my fiancé Cynthia. I've narrowed it down to a few individuals that may have something to do with it or may know something about it. I sent a few feelers out there and they served their purpose. I put the next phase of my plan in action.

Now, all that I have to do is sit back and see what the bait catches. It's going to take some time, but I'm a patient man. Once I find out who it is that murdered my future wife, I will make sure that they suffer. They won't even see it coming. Even the hardest individual has a soft spot.

I will find theirs and destroy them, psychologically, emotionally and then physically. They will feel like they've died long before I kill them. That's a promise.

Once I handle this situation, I plan on passing the baton to my protégé, G. G's been around me his entire life. His mother was one of my most profitable employees. Over two decades ago, she told me that she got caught up. One of the tricks impregnated her. I was heated. All that I could think about was how much money I was going to lose while she was pregnant. To my surprise, she still wanted to work throughout her pregnancy. There was definitely a market for pregnant pussy. She actually made me more money working while she was pregnant.

She lived with her son at one of my spots. As he grew up, he learned the game because he was around the game. Don't get me wrong, this boy had book smarts too. He went from daycare, to school, to college. He majored in business. When he graduated, we gave him a huge graduation party. I paid for his education as long as his mom kept working for me. She said that she was going to retire when he graduated. I told her that she should manage the girls instead. She wouldn't take my offer. She said she'd saved up enough money to take some time off for a few years and figure out what she wanted to do with this phase of her life.

When she quit, G didn't go to work in Corporate America, like his mother had hoped. He wanted to work for me. His mom was disappointed, but she knew it was inevitable. You can't grow up in this type of environment and not become a part of it on some level. I wanted him to keep his hands clean. So, I put him in charge of some of my legit businesses. He had to prove himself. First, I made him submit business plans to me on how he was going to grow the business. You see, I wanted to expand my businesses. Since G was now working for me, I wanted to see if that expensive ass degree paid off.

A few months after he graduated from college, his mother found out that she had breast cancer. She decided that she didn't want any radiation or chemotherapy. She said that she was tired and just wanted to live the rest of her days on her terms. I pleaded with her to reconsider. I even tried to guilt her into getting on treatment. I told her to think about her son. She told me that since the day she found out that she was pregnant, she lived her life for her son. She wanted him to have a better life, so she sacrificed hers. The sacrificing has come to an end. She said that she's earned her right to die in peace. I couldn't argue with her. I was going to miss her.

Before she passed away, she handed me an old tattered envelope. She told me to open it when she's passed on. I respected her wishes. When she died, I forgot all about the letter. It wasn't until a week later that I remembered that she gave it to me. When I opened it, my mouth dropped. I remember thinking to myself; *What the fuck?*

It was paternity test results. This shit said that G was my son! She handwrote on the document that she swabbed my cheek when I was asleep. That's how she got my sample. She also wrote that G already knows. I guess she had her reasons for keeping this info from me. All I can do now is continue to be the father I've always been for him. I'm not going to front. It felt good to know that he was mine.

Joan:

This guy is clearly hitting on me. I'm at the MAC counter working on inventory. This guy asks for my assistance with picking out eye shadow for his "sister". I know damn well that he isn't buying make up for his sister, but I play along.

"Hey Beautiful. Do you think you could recommend some nice eyeshadow for my sister?" he says to me smiling.

"Oh sure! Do you have a picture of your sister?" I ask to catch him in his lie.

"Actually, I do. We took a family picture this summer. Give me a sec to find it on my phone." He scrolls for about ten seconds and then hands me his phone.

"Which one is your sister?"

"She's the one standing in between my mom and dad. That's her in the red."

"She's beautiful. I know just the right shadows that would work with her coloring."

"Ok great. Pick a few out for me. I'm lost when it comes to make-up."

"My pleasure." I tell him. *Maybe he is getting it for his sister. He could still be lying. He could have found a picture of his sister, but is really buying it for his girlfriend.* I hand him three shades that will look great on his "sister".

"Those are pretty colors. I'm sure she'll love them. I'll be sure to tell her that a beautiful woman recommended them. Any chance that this beautiful woman is single? I'd love to go out for a drink to see if your outer beauty matches your inner beauty."

"I don't go out with customers. Sorry." He looks confused, but then smiles.

"Ok. Well pretty lady. You be sure to have a good night. Thanks again." He leaves.

I'm guessing that he has no clue that I'm transgender. I can't say I've been in a healthy relationship with a man ever. That's why I have no problem doing my night job. Those men know what they are getting. They know what they want. As unsafe as my behaviors are, I don't have to worry about the men being freaked out about me having a penis.

I'm working later than usual tonight at the mall. Thank God I saved up enough money to get a decent car. It may be a used car, but I ride around in this Ford Taurus like it's a new Benz. I don't have time to go home first and get my mind right for my night job. I'm hungry. Nothing is open that won't ruin my figure. I can starve until I get home in the morning or I can stop tripping and go get some fast food. I end up at Wendy's. I'm dressed too fly to be getting out of the car and walking into Wendy's. I opt for the drive-thru. Unfortunately, Everybody and their mama seems to be in the drive-thru line.

As I sit in the car waiting for my turn to order, I listen to the radio. They are playing non-stop love songs. I'm getting depressed listening to this stuff. I want someone to love me the way the singer is describing in his song. I don't know a lot of people transitioning. I don't know of any examples of transgender couples in a marriage. That's what I want for me. I want to be in a committed relationship. A few of the girls that I work with at night rely on social media to meet people. I don't like sharing my business on line. So, I don't mess with social media. I don't feel like I am missing out. From what I hear, everybody is on there lying anyway.

"Welcome to Wendy's, what can I get for you?"

"Hi. I'd like two value nuggets and value fries. I'd also like a bottle of water please."

114

"Will that be all?"

I'll take a man that will love me right if you've got one. "Yes, that's all. Thank you."

After I receive my food, I pull into a Wendy's parking space to eat in my car. I'm heated because they didn't give me any ketchup. I didn't ask for any, but they didn't ask me if I wanted any either. Why can't they just assume that I do? I'm not getting out of the car. If I wanted to get out of my car, I wouldn't have gone through drive-thru. I will just eat my fries without it.

I'm still torturing myself listening to love songs while eating my food. I'm not really as aware of my surroundings as I usually am. I'm caught up in my feelings. I'm feeling sorry for myself. I didn't ask to feel like a woman, but possess the body of a man. *Who would want that?* This makes me think that nobody will want me.

Knock Knock Knock!

The sound of someone knocking on my window scares the heck out of me. I roll down my window. I know my face looks irritated, but the face on the other side of the glass seems oblivious to it.

"Hey Beautiful! I saw you in my rearview mirror. I was in front of you in the drive-thru. I noticed you when you made your order. I actually heard your voice before I saw you. I knew that the voice was familiar. When I looked in my rearview and saw that it was you, I knew that it was meant to be."

"What was meant to be?" I say in a tone that suggests that I am busy and he is interrupting me.

"It was meant to be that I see you again. I see this as an opportunity to ask you out again, but not as a customer. I will never buy anything at MAC again if it allows me a chance to get to know you."

Shit. How do I respond to that? "I will say that you are persistent. You get knocked down and get right back up huh?"

"I didn't let your rejection knock me down. I just chalked it up as you didn't know any better." He says smirking.

"Oh, I didn't know any better huh? Well consider this your lucky night. I'm going to take you up on your offer. Let's meet this weekend for coffee."

"Coffee it is. So, Joan, are you a Dunkin Donuts or a Starbucks type of girl?' He says grinning hard.

"Definitely a Dunks girl. Are you going to tell me your name or am I supposed to guess?"

Laughing he says "I forgot I never told you my name. I obviously know yours because of the name tag you had on. I guess you would have known mine had I paid with credit."

"So, what is it?"

"Why don't we let that be a mystery. It will give you something to look forward to. I'll tell you my name if you show up for coffee."

"I just said that I would meet you. Is the suspense necessary?"

"Yes, it is Joan. I look forward to revealing my name to you this weekend. Will you meet me at the Dunkin Donuts in Copley? I like the scenery. How's Saturday at 11am?"

"Sure Stranger, I'll see you then."

"Have a good rest of your evening Joan." He walks back to his car. I watch to see which car he gets into. *Ok, he has a practical car.* He opens the door to a black Toyota Camry, gets in and pulls out. I don't want him to see me looking. So, I go back to eating. I wait for thirty seconds before looking up again. I smile. *God was listening.*

***

I stress myself out all day on Friday worrying about my coffee date. I wonder if he knows that I'm transgender. He doesn't look like the type that is into transgender women. Who am I fooling? I know he has no idea that I'm transgender. Do I tell him during coffee? Do I wait to see where this is going before I reveal that? Do I not show up and spare myself the humiliation? This shit shouldn't be so hard!

I arrive early. I am sitting at Dunks thirty minutes early. I'm still debating if I'm going to walk out and leave before he gets here. I get up to buy myself a hot chocolate instead of coffee. Nobody is in line.

"May I have a medium hot chocolate, no whip cream."

"Make that two please." The voice behind me says.

I turn around to see my date, The Stranger, standing with a huge grin and flowers. *He bought flowers…roses.*

117

He orders an assorted box of munchkins to go along with our hot chocolates. He gives me the flowers and a miniature card is affixed to them. I'm completely taken off guard by his sweet gesture. I walk back to a table located at the far end of the shop, away from the door. I have my back to the door. I don't want to see any openly opinionated people show their disgust for me with hateful looks. I don't want anything to mess this date up.

Why does he keep grinning? "It's good to see you Beautiful."

"Is that my name now? You don't like the name Joan?"

"I love the name Joan. It's a classy name. I like how you light up when I call you Beautiful. You don't light up when I call you Joan. I'm gonna stick with Beautiful."

Somebody pinch me. "Ok, I wish I had a name to call you. I guess I'll continue to call you Stranger."

"Stranger it is." He says laughing. "Coming from you it doesn't sound so bad."

"Is that so?" Now, I'm smiling.

"So, Beautiful, what's your favorite eye shadow color?"

"That's a random question. Why are you asking me that?"

Grinning, he says "Because when you were so passionate about getting my sister the right eye shadow, it made me wonder what colors you felt went with your coloring. I figure we can start out by learning the little things about each other and then work our way up to the big things. Sound good?"

"Sounds good to me Stranger." I'm grinning.

Today was the best day I've had in a long time. The date was great! We took the opportunity to learn about the little things. That took the pressure that I was feeling away. My anxiety disappeared. I felt free to be me. We agreed to meet again next Saturday, same place and time. I can't wait.

As I sit in my kitchen and replay the date over and over inside of my head, I look at the roses he gave me. These are the first roses that I've ever received from a man. I plan to put them in a vase that I have filled with fake flowers. It felt good to have real flowers to replace the fake ones with.

The small card affixed to the roses falls on the table when I take the roses out of their paper to place in the vase. I'll look at it in a second. I need to put some water inside of the vase. As I'm sitting down admiring the roses, I pick up the card to see what The Stranger wrote. The card reads:

Roses represent beauty. They remind me of you. Hope you enjoyed the date as much as I know that I will;)

Stranger no more…Jonathan Christian

When I initially read the card all I read was "Jonathan". I thought that he knew my name. Then I read it again. He signed it as Jonathan Christian. That's not my name. What are the odds of meeting a man that has the same name? I almost wish he knew that my name was Jonathan. That would mean that he knew what I was packing.

We haven't gotten romantic. I am making a conscious decision to not bring up my past until things look like they are taking a turn to something more physical. I don't want to do anything pass giving him a hug. If he ends up being a man that is disgusted by me being transgender, having hugged me won't mess with his head as much as kissing me would.

This is a tough life to live. Being a black transgender pre-op woman is stressful! There are so many things that I have to consider that other women don't. Ordinary every day activities can be overwhelming a lot of the time. Simple shit like, what bathroom to use filled me with anxiety in high school. Going to the urologist becomes humiliating as soon as I walk through the door. Most stare at me with a look of confusion. Then when they add one plus one, the confused stares morph into stares of hate and disgust. Filling out forms that ask for your gender and always being told that I filled it out wrong. Then having to tell them that I have a penis makes me want to shrink inside of myself.

There are days when I hate myself. I stand in the mirror naked and hate the thing that reminds me of who the world says that I am. That is not who I am. I am a beautiful woman. I've never been a man. I may have male sex organs but I've never been a man. I've asked myself so many times why I have to live this life of suffering. Many times, I thought about taking a nap and making sure that I didn't wake up from it.

My Mom was always there for me during the low points. Her words always helped me. It's crazy because she didn't even know that those were the words that I needed to hear. She's gone now and I don't have anyone to provide any words of encouragement. How could they? I don't share my feelings to even allow someone to be there for me. I thought that Karma was different. I could talk to her. But, she messed things up when she asked to sleep with me. We all have our issues. I'm not judging her, but she has definitely disappointed me. I'm going to give her another chance though. I've decided that I am not going to ask her to help me with my surgery. I will figure out a way to make it happen.

Eve:

I never imagined I'd be feeling Greg as much as I am. It's like God knew that I was craving companionship, worthwhile companionship and he delivered him to me. Richard hurt me. I really loved him. I saw us building a life together. Yet, it seems I was the only one that was banking on a future together. He moved on rather quickly after our breakup. He didn't even try salvage our relationship. I think that hurt the most. He thought that I wasn't worth the trouble.

Fuck you Richard! Greg is proving himself to be quite the catch. He's attentive, sexy, supportive, encouraging and wants to be in a committed relationship. He wants a big family one day. So, do I. He's even talked about me going to Boston with him to meet his family. It's only been a few weeks, but he may be *The One.*

I thought Richard was the best I've ever had in bed. I didn't know what I was missing. Greg knows how to satisfy me on a level that Richard didn't. He talks to me. He makes love to me mentally before he does physically. That right there is what separates the boys from the men. Greg is a man. Greg is The Man. I'm proud to say that he is my man.

Helen's been giving me additional dirty looks since she figured out Greg and I were seeing each other. I just smile at her. She's such a hater. I got a week to go before I take my pen back. I walk by her desk each morning to make sure that it is still where I left it. Thirty days is enough time for her to slip up. If it is happening anywhere near her cubicle, I will have footage next week. I can't wait to review the tape.

Angel has been on a war path. She's been fighting with her child's father since they went to court. She thought that she won because the judge ordered that her child's father have money deducted from his pay every two weeks. The messed-up part is that when it was determined what he would be paying for child support, he ended up having to pay less than he had voluntarily been giving her. Had she left well enough alone, she would have eventually gone back to receiving the $850 a month. Now she only gets $600.

Every morning I listen to her talk shit about her Ex. Here's what I think. I think she needs some new dick. She needs a distraction because she is too consumed with this man. To help distract her, I offer to go out with her to the club this weekend. She accepts. Hopefully, she'll find a cutie to take up some of the down time that she uses obsessing over her Ex. She is too fly to be acting bitter. I need her to get it together.

Gina and I have been getting along, better than we ever did while I was growing up. Finally, everything seems to be coming together. Besides my hater, things are good at work. Things are good with my home life and things are great with my love life. Karma and I had a long talk before she left to go back to Boston. I promised to trust her more; she promised to be there for me. She also promised to never share our secret. I have no choice but to trust her.

I told her about Greg. She told me that I was acting thirsty. She said that I needed to get control before I give up control and that I "need to have the upper hand". I can't help the way that I feel about him. Each day I spend with Greg is better than the day before. You don't know how bad you had it until someone shows you how good you can have it. I never saw this coming. He spoils me to the point that I can't help but to love him. I am definitely becoming attached to this man. Although, I try not to show it too much.

I find myself planning things in my mind for us. I think about a future with him. I've even imagined what it would be like to have kids with him. My crazy behind has already gone into David's Bridal to try on dresses. I will admit; it's getting out of hand. I need to pull it together. He is just a man. I'm acting like I never had a man before. If he saw this side of me, he'd probably be scared off.

Instead, I heed Karma's advice. I try not to get too excited about seeing him, in his presence. I make sure that I don't bother him while we are at work. The only time we have lunch together is when he invites me. That's not because I am cheap. It is because I don't want to appear to be too eager. *The games women must play to keep a good man.*

***

A week has flown by. This morning I am going to retrieve my pen from Helen's desk. It is going to kill me all day having to wait until I get home to see what is on the tape. I'm not going to go out of my way to expose whatever it is that I find, but I will keep it in the "just in case a bitch wants to act cute" bank. I'll have something to hold over her head if she does.

It's Friday. It's pay day. Tonight, Angel and I are going out. I can't wait. I haven't been out since I've been back in town. The last time that I went to a club in Charlotte, I had a run in

123

with my ex best friend Lynne. It really wasn't a run in. I was ready for her. Since she liked messing with dicks from my past so much, I beat her down with a dildo in the parking lot of the club. Thinking back to that night, that shit was funny. We both went to jail that night. It was a crazy night and one that I don't want to repeat. Jail is not for me.

Angel and I decided to make an event out of our night. She has her Ex watching their kid. After work, we are going to the mall a to buy outfits for tonight and to get something to eat before going out. I'm really looking forward to it. She mentioned that she wanted to go to Tempo. I figure *what the hell.* I'm not banned from Tempo any more. *I don't think.* I learned my lesson and have no plans on fighting anyone in the club. I'm too sexy to be acting that way.

We arrive at the club looking like we are Basketball Wives on the reunion episode. We are seriously doing the most. Angel said she wanted to feel good, better than good. She wanted to dress for her mood not the occasion. I agreed to follow suit. I couldn't have my girl up in the club looking snobby without me. I'm sure we were going to get more looks from the women than the men.

As we walk into the club, the bouncer stops us to pat us down. He then looks through our clutch bags. While this is going on, I can feel the hate coming from two sisters standing outside of the bathroom. They are looking at us like we did something to them in a past life. I don't feed into it. Like I said before, I'm not trying to go back to jail for beating a bitch's ass. Angel, on the other hand, doesn't look like she's willing to tap into that self-control I told her to have tonight.

"Where the fuck do they think they are going?" one of the haters says softly to her girl.

I hear it, but I decide to let it go. I wasn't sure if Angel heard them. I can't say that I didn't feel like a punk letting them slide, but sometimes being an adult about things doesn't feel good. I want to act like a junior high school girl that just found out someone was talking shit behind her back.

"Did they just say something smart to us Eve?" Angel asks and looks at me with a pissed look on her face.

"Girl, just keep walking. We have a table reserved in VIP. Let the bathroom groupies hate from afar." I say this, but I'm feeling the same way Angel is. I'm ready to check these bitches.

"Ok, I'll let them slide for now. I know you don't want to go to jail, but I got a lot of anger I need to get out with everything that I have going on. Providing a beat down might just be what the doctor ordered."

"Girl, dick is what the doctor ordered. Keep it together. No men are going to step to you if you're up in here acting ghetto. The ones that do, you'll want to steer clear away from. Let's make it to our table in peace and have a few drinks."

"You're right. I'll chill. I just need some male attention. If the females are hating on me this much, I know that I'll be getting a lot of attention from the men. That's why they are mad. They are scared that we are gonna take the attention off of them. Damn. Now I kind of feel sorry for them. I'll be sure to send the men I discard over to their table. Wait. They don't have a table. I'll be sure to send them over to the bathroom where they'll be." Angel is cracking up as she says this. I'm cracking up right along with her.

A new song by Chris Brown comes on. I can't help but get up out of my seat and dance. Angel joins me. We leave our tables and enter the general population on the dance floor. We both dance like we are the baddest chicks in Chris Brown's video. Angel is a sexy dancer. When

125

I dance, I make sure that I look cute but I don't have the sexy dance thing going for me the way Angel does.

Angel is touching herself and swaying her body. All eyes are on us, but they are really on her. I stay in my lane. I am dancing cute. I'm looking back at myself while I'm dancing. I have my mouth pursed like something is sour. I'm in my zone. Angel, on the other hand, is biting her bottom lip and doing a stripper-like routine. *Shit*. All she needs is a pole. I'm going to ask her where she got all of those moves from when we go back to the table. Suddenly I'm dancing with a man that is not on the same beat as me. He is messing up my rhythm.

There are two men sandwiching Angel. She looks like she's being molested the way she's letting them feel all over her. I ain't mad. Whatever she needs to stop obsessing over her Ex is fine with me. Once the Chris Brown song goes off, I go back to the table and relax my feet. I don't want my feet to start hurting. It is still early. I'll have a funky disposition if my feet hurt. That will mess up my entire night.

I expect Angel to get off of the dance floor after a song or two. After the third song, I realize that she is going to probably stay out there for the rest of the night. I'm happy for her. She's getting a bunch of attention. I'm sure that she will leave with a half of a dozen new contacts added to her phone.

I get a text from Greg. He asks how things are going? I tell him that I'm just chilling in VIP while Angel turns up. The next texts says 'COME OUTSIDE.' I want to ask why, but I motion to Angel that I'll be right back. I take both of our pocket books with me. I'm shocked and pleased to see Greg outside.

126

He gets out and opens his passenger side door for me. I get in. He walks around the front of his car to get in. He then pulls off to the far end of the parking lot and parks. He doesn't shut the car off. *I guess he's not coming in the club. What did he come here for?*

"You look nice young lady."

"Thank you young man. What are you doing here?" I ask with a hint of confusion on my face.

"I figured you'd be in the club letting some random dude dry hump you. I didn't want you to forget what I give you. I didn't want you to forget how my mouth feels while it makes love to your pussy. I didn't want you to forget how my fingers feel on your clit when I tease you. I didn't want you to forget what this dick can do for you." He says while pulling out his dick and stroking it.

I'm wet just by listening to him. All I want is to sit on his dick. It looks really good as he's stroking it. I want to wrap my mouth around it. He takes his hand off of his dick and there's pre-cum on his finger tip. He puts his hand up my dress and pushes my thong to the side. Then he takes his wet finger and rubs it on my clit. I'm losing it now.

"You better had brought a condom because I'm fucking you in this car right now."

"Oh, you want this dick right now? You want to ride this dick in my car. You don't care that people might see us that are walking to their cars. You want them to see me sucking on your titties while I let you ride this dick. You want them to see me get you to climax like no other man has done before? You want them to hear you moan from the intense pleasure I'm going to give you? Is that what you want?"

That did it. I didn't even wait for him to put the condom on. I sat right on his dick and rode him for a good three minutes before I came. He came after me. I am his. This man is too good to be true. Who comes to the club to fuck his girlfriend and then sends her back in the club to think about him the rest of the night. I don't know if that's game or not but I definitely fell for it. When I get back into the club. Angel is still on the dance floor. She's sweaty now. Her hair is curly at the roots. She straightened her hair, but it is slowly going back to its natural curly form.

I enjoy the rest of my night in VIP people watching and drinking wine. Angel had a good time and I had a great time. Shortly after I got back into the club from being outside with Greg, he sent me a text that said 'DROP HER OFF AND COME OVER SO YOU CAN COME AGAIN.' I couldn't wait for the club to be over so that I could drop Angel off.

Karma:

BJ is obviously mad at me. She left out of my couples' session without saying a word. She didn't call me later that day. I didn't call her either. I know her. She will avoid me for a little while and then seek me out. So, I'll just wait on her. She'll come around. I don't know what the big deal was. It is not like I asked her to join us. I do feel kind of bad though. I'm sure she got a little jealous watching me with a man. She knows I don't discriminate. Sex is sex.

Later today, I'm having dinner at my grandmother's house. She wanted to meet with me before, but I was in Charlotte. It seemed like it was important, but by the end of the conversation she made it sound like it could wait. I wonder what she wants. I can't imagine she blew through all the money I put into her account. I guess I'll find out later.

I am on my way home from the airport, when the taxi driver calls himself taking a short cut. It is not a short cut. We get caught up in local traffic when we should have stayed on the highway. I am getting aggravated. I am ready to be home already. As I look out of the window, I notice a tattoo shop that I'd never seen before. It is new. That spot used to be a Dominican barbershop.

I'm tired of sitting in traffic and I'm curious so I tell the driver to let me out. I pay my fare and take my carry-on bag out of the trunk myself. Traffic wasn't going anywhere, but the car behind the taxi had the nerve to beep, like I was holding things up. I ignore him. After pulling out my luggage, I make sure to shut the trunk of the taxi in a slow exaggerated fashion. Then I turn around and smile at the dumb ass person that honked the horn.

"Hi! Welcome to As Mighty as The Pen. What can I do for you today?"

"You have a great smile." *She's sexy.*

'Thank you. Are you looking to get a tattoo today?" She says blushing.

"I guess I am. Do I need to make an appointment or do you take walk-ins?"

"I just finished my last client for the day, but Tracy is free right now."

"No offense, but I'll make an appointment with you when you are available." *She has dimples.*

"No offense taken. Well, why don't you tell me what kind of tattoo that you are thinking about getting? I have time for a consult. Then we can get you scheduled for a later date. Sound good to you?"

129

Looks good to me. "Sure, that sounds good. Let's consult." I call a cab to pick me up in thirty minutes from the tattoo shop.

Tori is her name. She may not have agreed to tattoo me today, but she agreed to see me tonight. She is meeting me at my condo after I have dinner with my grandmother. I have an hour to get to Milton.

***

It's starting to rain outside. It feels raw outside. The rain is making it feel colder than it really is. I need to put some air in my tire. The tire light is lit up on my dashboard screen and I see that the driver's side front tire is low. This is not the day that I want to be out in the rain putting air in my tire.

Since I'm at the gas station, I decide to fill up my tank. The credit card swipe at the gas station is out of order. There's a yellow piece of construction paper written in marker that says to see the cashier. I really don't feel like going inside, but all of the other gas spots are taken. I have no choice.

When I get to the cashier counter, I grab some Dentyne gum. I love the taste of cinnamon. The cashier doesn't address me. I can see that she is busy, but I can also see that she knows I'm here. All she has to do is acknowledge me and tell me that she'll be right with me. She doesn't do it.

I'm looking at her and dissecting her. I instinctively size her up. *Blue collar female, in her forties, with heroine user teeth, a crackhead physique with Salvation Army attire. She's a religious zealous.* She looks a mess. Her t-shirt reads GOD IS PRO LIFE. I feel an attitude building inside of me. She's white. I know that shouldn't even matter, but right now, I'm feeling like we are in the 1950's and she thinks she ain't got to show the same respect to the darkies as she does to her white customers. At the end of the day, rude is rude.

I'm about to cuss this woman the hell out, but she finally addresses me. She doesn't say I'm sorry. She just asks if that will be all. I'm looking at her like *"No Bitch. This isn't all. I owe you an ass whoopin."* Instead, I say "yes" and ask her to put $40 on pump number six. I can't stand ignorant ass people. If you deal with customers for a living, it's a prerequisite that you have customer service skills. She may want to work on acquiring some skills that will get her a better job than a gas station clerk.

This detour is definitely going to make me late getting to Milton. I text my grandmother to let her know that I am running late. She takes punctuality very seriously. If I'm not early, I'm late in her eyes. I'm finished filling up my gas tank. I get into my car and go inside of the arm rest. That is where I keep my wet wipes. I use the wet wipes on my hand. Then I use a new one on my steering wheel. Those gas pumps have all types of germs. That's why I usually go to a full-service station.

I am late. The rain makes the commute to Milton even longer. Folks just don't know how to drive. They become especially challenged when it's raining out. John Legend's album played from beginning to end. I'm still not as close as I thought I would be by now. I decide to switch John Legend and listen to some India Arie. I need to be in a positive space when I get to my grandmother's house. India will put me there.

I've listened to four songs on her album. The fifth one is about to begin, but I cut it off. I'm here. There's an extra car in the drive way. It's a silver Honda Accord. I think it is Rochelle's car. My mom can't stand Rochelle; well, *couldn't stand Rochelle*. Damn. That quickly, my mood changes. I think about my mom and the fucked-up way that she died. I lost my dad too, but that was different. He wasn't my primary care-taker growing up. She was. Ava had some dysfunctional ways about her, but there's no doubt that she loved me. Growing up she'd always say "All I do, I do for you." I miss her.

"Change your face. Why are you looking all sad and shit?"

This is how you greet me? "Hi. I didn't realize my face looked that way. What's for dinner?"

"You'll see as soon as you bring your late behind into the kitchen." She says while hugging me.

"Sorry about that. I didn't give myself enough time and didn't factor in the rain."

"Child, you know that the rain has folks acting like they are handicap Asian women drivers. You should have given yourself extra, extra time. Anyway, you are here now. Let's go into the kitchen. By the way, Rochelle is having dinner with us too."

Rochelle is drinking wine. She sips it with her pinky pointed out. Folks these days' act bougie without having the money to qualify them to be bougie. I'd bet money that most of the folks that use the word, don't even know that that word derives from the Black Bourgeoisie. They are the group of Blacks that looked down on other Blacks who hadn't attained the wealth or status that they have. Being a part of the Bourgeoisie wasn't a positive thing; at least not from the eyes of the other Blacks that weren't a part of the group. Folks today use it recklessly. I may not have gone to college, but Ava made sure I knew my shit, especially if it pertained to Black people.

Before heading to the kitchen table, I announce that I am going to use the bathroom first. I need to pee and wash my hands for dinner. As I walk down the hall, I see pictures of my mom and myself. These pictures weren't on the walls before. I'm very surprised to see that my grandmother has pictures of us up.

I open the bathroom door and see the toilet. All of a sudden, I have to go pee immediately. Just the sight of the toilet has me with my hand between my legs holding myself so that nothing slips out. I make it to the toilet in time. When I let loose, the sound of my pee hitting the toilet water sounds like someone has the water faucet on high. It doesn't sound like a woman peeing.

It takes over a minute to empty my bladder. I really have to stop holding my pee so long. After I'm done, I sit on the toilet for a while. I think about my day so far. Early this morning, I was in Richard's bed. By afternoon, I am back in Massachusetts plotting to get this tattoo artist in my bed. There's no doubt about it; I am not a one-man--or woman--girl. I don't know who I thought that I was fooling when I was trying to become Richard's brother's housewife. I don't think I'm built to be in a monogamous relationship.

Don't get me wrong. I thought that Ray was perfect for me. He is ambitious. He is wealthy. He is sexy. There were just two things wrong. He didn't want sex as much as I did and he didn't want me having sex with anyone other than him. We were destined to fail. I look at the scar on my right hand from when I stabbed myself. I smile as I think about how that quick

thinking got his ass locked up. I framed him. He deserved it though. He hit me, but he didn't stab

me. I bet he will think twice before putting his hands on a woman again.

When it hit me that our relationship was over, I was upset at first. It turned out to be a

blessing. One door shut and many windows opened. I never would have met my match if things

worked out with Ray. His brother Richard is the only man that I've met that has the same sex

drive as I do. I do have a little guilt for messing with my sister's ex-boyfriend. But, at least he

isn't her current boyfriend. That would be worse.

I'm not in a relationship with Richard. We just use each other to get our sexual needs

met. That's why it was an easy decision to abort his baby. I didn't even tell him that I was

pregnant. There was no need to. I wasn't going to keep the baby of my ex-boyfriend's brother,

who also is my sister's ex-boyfriend. That would be so scandalous. Richard and I both vowed not

to tell our siblings or each other's sibling about our arrangement. It is our secret.

My grandmother must think that I am in her bathroom blowing it up. I've been in here for

longer than it takes to go pee. I'm immediately grossed out when I get to the sink. I have this

thing about hair. I don't want to see anyone's DNA in sinks, tubs, toilets on the floor or in my

food. If you notice that a strand of your hair fell in the sink, be kind and rinse it down the drain.

Nobody wants to have to wash hair out of the sink; especially when it is not theirs. The hair is

red. It is not my grandmother's hair. She wouldn't leave hair in the sink. It is her friend

Rochelle's. *No home training.*

"You sure were in the bathroom for a while. Are you ok." Rochelle asks when I reenter

the kitchen. *My grandmother's name is Claudia, not Rochelle. Mind your business.*

134

"I'm ok thanks for asking. So, ladies, what's for dinner? I'm starved."

"Chicken, broccoli and ziti with a side of garlic bread." Claudia answers.

"I'll set the table. Let's go and sit down. I'm starving too." Rochelle says.

Why is she ordering us around like this is her house? "Ok" I say and sit down.

"Why did you want to have dinner? You sounded like you wanted to talk." I say addressing my grandmother. She doesn't respond immediately. She takes a gulp of her wine, while Rochelle has her face in her plate. Something is up. My grandmother speaks.

"There's no way around it. I've never been one to shoot the shit or beat around the bush. So, I'll just get right to it. I'm sick, Karma. I have dementia. I've seen a doctor. I'm not getting any better. I just started taking meds that will hopefully slow down the progression. Rochelle will be living with me to make sure I stay on point. I'm not moving back in with you so don't ask. I don't want you having to take care of your grandmother. I want you to live your life. That's it."

I don't know what to say. So, she's not dying. She's just forgetting shit. Well that's not so bad. I don't think I can handle losing my mother, father and grandmother in the same year. It's all making sense now. When she was asking me for my mother, she was being serious. I thought she was just fucking with me. She really forgot that her daughter died. This is a little more than her just forgetting where she left her glasses or her keys.

That's why this bitch is in here acting like she's running the show. She will be running the show soon. I don't know how comfortable I am with this. Rochelle is not family. My grandmother should move back in with me.

"Why won't you move back in with me? Wouldn't you want to be with family? No offense Rochelle, but I barely know you. What I have heard about you was from my mother. We both know how she felt about you. I don't' know how comfortable I am with this."

"When you get gray pussy hairs you might have something to say worth considering. Until then, you are way too young to be deciding what is right and wrong for me. I was just letting you know out of courtesy. I am not here asking for your permission. I'm losing my mind and you are here talking about what you feel comfortable with. You sure are Ava's child."

"Damn, why do you have to come at me like that? I'm just trying to be there for you. If you'd prefer your BFF to take care of you, fine. I can't stop you. Do what you want." I have a slight attitude.

"Change your tone when you talk to me bitch. You are talking to your momma's momma."

I'm quiet for the remainder of the meal. My grandmother and Rochelle chat it up like I'm not even in the room. There was no more talk about her dementia and what that means for the family or for her going forward. I guess I'm just supposed to check in with Rochelle to see about my grandmother.

I planned on staying longer, but I'm ready to go. I give both of them hugs goodbye and tell them that I have plans that I don't want to be late for. My grandmother looks at me likes she wants to tell me that I didn't put that much importance on getting to her house on time. She doesn't say it. She doesn't have to. I can read her. She says goodbye and that she'll be in touch. I text Tori as I'm walking to my car.

BJ:

What's that saying? *When one door closes, another door opens*. I went out the night after the pornographic counselling session Karma had me involved in. That night, I met Vi. We hit it off and have been seeing each other every day since then. I haven't even had the urge to call Karma. Normally, by now, I would have tried to call her. I guess I'm over her. It feels good to say that. Vi is beautiful. She's exotic. She's good with her hands in and out of the bed. She's an artist.

Gay and Lesbian people joke about how quickly we get in and out of relationships. We do, so there is *some* truth to it. At least the young ones do. Vi is my girlfriend. She is so kind. And is very attentive. She looks out for me. Throughout the day she checks on me just to see how I'm doing. When we kiss, it is so sensual. I melt. She is so sexy. When I first saw her naked, I was mesmerized by her nipple ring. It is a canary yellow diamond loop on her left nipple. It looks so pretty against her big brown succulent nipple.

She sleeps here at night. She doesn't live here, but she's been coming over every day after work. She is usually here like clockwork every night. Except for one night last week--she was later than usual. She told me that she had a new client so that's why she was late. I believe her. She has no reason to lie.

Tonight, I'm making dinner for us. I make rice, beans and chicken with a side of avocado. She told me that it is her favorite; *she is my favorite*. She is becoming my everything. I will cook for her every day if she wants me to. I will bring her breakfast in bed. I will pack a lunch for her to take to work. She'll never go hungry.

Sometimes she goes out with her work friends. I went with them once and didn't really enjoy myself. They are too free spirited for me. Vi asked me to go out with them again and I declined. I told her that I didn't feel comfortable. I felt like and outsider. I'd prefer that she go out with her work friends without me. She stopped asking after I told her that.

Last night was one of those nights. She went out with her work friends and didn't come back until four o'clock in the morning. The clubs close at two o'clock. I guess they got something to eat after. She tells me not to wait up for her, but I can't help it. I worry about her and want to make sure that she's ok. I want to hold her while we sleep. I have gotten so used to sleeping with her; it's hard to rest without her. I've become attached to her.

I spoon her when she gets in the bed. That smell; she smells like a perfume that I know all too well. I tense up because my body is reacting to the smell instead of to the feel of my lover beside me. I feel guilty. She turns around and kisses me. She's kissing me and I'm thinking about Karma. I try to shake thoughts of Karma off but it's not working. My body is responding to Vi's touch, but not for the right reasons. Karma is not going to mess this relationship up for me. It's like she put some type of spell on me. She's probably somewhere sleeping with her next conquest.

Karma:

When I left my grandmother's house, I was in a funky mood. Tori was just what I needed. She made me forget all about the stress I was feeling. She is officially on the roster. I ran into that dude I slept with from the club at the Prudential Mall. I forgot all about him. I put him back on the roster too. I plan on seeing him tonight. Richard called me. He says that he wants to see me. I'm not rushing out to Charlotte; I just came back. He's going to have to come to Massachusetts if he wants some of this.

I spoke to Joan. We made up. I agreed to stop propositioning her. I also agreed to focus on our friendship and not her dick. I will admit; I am very curious, but I'll find someone else to complete that task on my sexual bucket list. Joan filled me in on some new guy that she met. She said that she is falling for him, but hasn't done anything past hugging him.

How could you fall for someone that you haven't sampled yet? She tells me that she hasn't kissed him because she hasn't disclosed that she is a trans woman. Joan explained her logic behind not kissing him. She said that if he kisses her without knowing that she's a trans woman, it could be detrimental to her health once he learns the truth.

I told her to stop wasting time and just tell him. She said that she's not ready and she's enjoying her time so much that she doesn't want it to end. She'll find the right time. Hopefully, it is before he puts his hands up her skirt. I'm going to stay out of that. This is unfamiliar territory for me. If she thinks she should wait to tell him, then she should wait.

I texted BJ. I had to give it to her. I thought for sure that she'd be the first one to reach out. In my text, I asked her if she was ok. She replied by writing that she is in a committed

139

relationship and she'd appreciate it if I no longer contacted her. When I read that, I remember thinking to myself that she works quickly. How could she be in a committed relationship that soon? Either she met someone as clingy as she is or she has no clue and she's the only one in her so called "committed relationship".

That's why she and I can only be friends. I had to take her off the roster. She is too damn clingy. I like her as a person; she's a good person. When she told me that she loved me, I knew I had to fall back. I gave her no reason to love me. I gave her orgasms. That's about it. Either way, I'm happy she found someone to share her time with. Speaking of finding someone. I need to call Eve.

"Hello"

"Why you acting like you don't have caller ID? You know who it is."

She laughs. "Hello Karma. How are you this evening?"

"Oh, we're feeling proper tonight? I'm well. And you?"

"I'm in love."

"Did you just say that you are in love?"

"Yup. I sure did." I can tell she has a wide grin on her face.

"You remember what I told you before. Make sure you have the upper hand. Does he love you more than you love him? I hope so. Please don't tell me that you said you love him first. Did you?'

"Karma, what does that matter? I'm telling you that I am in love. Be happy for me!"

"I am happy for you. I just don't want to see you get hurt. That's all" I say sincerely.

"Don't worry. He is not Richard. He's a way better man than Richard. I don't even miss Richard. He can sleep with the entire East Coast for all I care. I am so over him."

Massachusetts is on the East Coast. "Well good for you. I'm proud of you."

She told me about how he came to the club and did her in the car. I didn't see what was so special about getting done in a car, but I didn't judge her. Now if she said that he came to get her after the club and bent her over the trunk of his car and did her in public while the club was letting out: then I'd be impressed.

What she says next shocks the shit out of me.

"Karma, I'm pregnant and I'm keeping it."

Did this bitch just say she's keeping it? "What?"

"Yes, you heard me right. I am pregnant."

"You being pregnant isn't what is shocking. The fact that you are going to keep it is what floored me. Are you sure? Have you thought this through? What did he say when you told him?"

"I didn't tell him yet. You are the first person that I told. I got a blood test. I wanted to make sure that I really was pregnant before mentioning it. I plan on telling him soon."

"When is soon? This all feels like it is happening so quickly. Didn't you just meet him?"

"I know you're just worrying out of love. I appreciate your concern, but I got this. Just be happy for me Karma."

"I'm sorry. I'm just protective. If you are happy then I'm happy. This new man of yours better be grateful too. When are you going to send me a picture of him? I'd like to see who my nephews father is going to be."

"He doesn't like pictures and he's not on social media. I'll get one soon enough. When I do, I'll send it to you."

That's game right there. He doesn't like pictures and he's not on social media. This dude definitely has something to hide. Eve's so caught up in love that she didn't recognize game. Game recognizes game. As soon as she sends me his picture, I'm going to research his shady ass. Damn. I feel bad. She's pregnant. She's about to get her heart broken again and now she'll have a baby to remind her of the heart ache.

Eve's in love. BJ's in love. Joan's falling in love. I must've missed the memo. They can go ahead with all that love mess. It requires way too much energy and effort. I'm not ready for that yet. I got too many things on my sexual bucket list to take care of. Love would get in the way of me accomplishing those things.

Joan:

Every date that I've had with Jonathan has been great. I can tell that there is some sexual tension building between us. I still haven't let him kiss me. I still haven't told him my secret. I will admit, it feels weird calling him Jonathan. I thought I put that name behind me, but here it is sneaking its way back into my life.

I've decided that I am going to tell him tonight. I thought about a few ways to tell him. I want to break it to him gently. I can't decide if I should do it at the restaurant where there are people around. There's safety in doing it in a public space. I also thought that it's something that we should talk about in the privacy of his home. He hasn't shown any violent traits and there have been no red flags.

We haven't talked about any issues where I could gage how he feels about LGBTQ issues. Maybe, I'll bring some up tonight when we meet for dinner. That way, I'll be able to determine his potential response to my secret. I think that I will tell him about Thanksgiving's at my grandmother's house. I'll mention cousin Gary and see how he responds.

***

"You look great as usual Joan."

"Thanks Jonathan." *I feel like I'm talking to myself when I say his name - our name.*

"I was hoping that you might want to come over tonight after dinner. We could watch a movie or something. Does that sound like something you are up for?

"Let's play it by ear." *He wants to take it to the next level.*

"Play it by ear? We've been on a lot of dates Joan. You always want to meet in public places. You never let me pick you up in my car so that we can ride together. You give off vibes

143

like you are feeling me, but you won't let me even kiss you to show you that I am feeling you. What's up with you? Are we in the friend zone and I just didn't catch on?"

"That all depends on you." I say hesitantly.

"It all depends on me? It's more like it all depends on you. I want to kiss you Joan. Will you let me kiss you?"

"Jonathan. *There goes that name again.* I really like you …"

"But…" Jonathan says without letting me finish.

"There are no buts. I need to tell you something about myself and I'm afraid."

"Damn Joan. It can't be that bad. What is it? Are you a stripper? Are you a felon? Are you HIV positive? Are you married? I know that you're not gay because you wouldn't waste my time. So, what is it? If it is not any of the things I've mentioned, I can't imagine that anything that you'd say would make me feel any differently about you."

"It's none of the things you mentioned. It's a little more complicated than …"

He cut me off, kissing me before I got the chance to tell him. *Shit! Shit! Shit!* This is not how things were supposed to go down. I saw his lips coming close to mine, but, I didn't stop him. The truth is, I wanted it. I wanted to kiss him. That kiss may cost me. He kissed me and slid his tongue in my mouth. A smooch might not have been something he couldn't shake off, but he put his tongue in my mouth. If he doesn't take my disclosure well, that French kiss is going to be hard for him to shake off.

"Jonathan, you've just made this a lot harder than I hoped it would be. I'm just going to get this over with. I planned on handling this delicately, but there's no way to do that now. I'm a trans woman."

He looks confused. That's better than the look of disgust that I was expecting.

"I am a transgender woman."

"What the fuck do you mean?" *This is the first time I've heard him curse.*

"I was born a male. I take hormones to look this way."

"What the fuck are you trying to tell me Joan?"

"I'm not trying to tell you anything. I'm telling you that I'm not fully a woman yet physically. I still have a penis." I watch him for a reaction. *Maybe I should have worded that different and said that I don't have a vagina.*

He sits in silence for about ten seconds. Then he jumps out of his seat and puts his hands around my neck. A male patron intervenes pulling him off of me. Then someone else intervenes and drags him out of the restaurant. Jonathan screams.

"You guys got it all wrong. I'm not a woman beater! She's a fucking man. I should be able to beat his ass like a man!"

The owner of the restaurant threatens to call the police. Jonathan leaves without causing any more trouble. I am humiliated. Tears are falling from my eyes. I'm crying. I knew this would be the outcome. Who was I fooling thinking anyone could love me? I don't even love me.

Craig:

I ran into Lance's ex-husband Javier. He looked like shit. He fell off. He wasn't the well-groomed dude I knew when he was married to Ava's bestie Lance. He looked like a scrub. I ran into him outside of the barbershop. He needed to come in and get a cut, but instead he was going into the convenience store next door.

"What's up Javier? Long time no see brother."

"Heeeey Craig. Yes, it has been a long time."

"I was about to get a line-up, but I can't pass up this opportunity to catch up. Walk with me down the street to the bar. Let's have drink."

Javier knew that he didn't have a choice. Telling me no would bring on the type of problems from me he didn't want to have.

There's nothing like a stiff drink between men. Javier is a loose lipped drunk. He told me what happened the night that Ava and Ben died. He told me that he is the one that stabbed Ben to death. He also told me that Ben was on some drugs or something because he was out of it and couldn't fight back. He also said he thinks he peed on himself because he smelled like urine. Everything was starting to make sense.

Ava used to joke with me and say if she gets mad enough she's going to get back at Ben herself. She said that she'd use the same drug he used on her and pee on him. She would laugh it off, but I know my cousin. There's always some truth to her jokes. I don't know if she carried it out exactly like that, but it sounds like it was very close. *Damn, Ava, why didn't you tell me you were going over there that day?*

I planted a bomb in Ben's car. I expected the man that disfigured Ava's face to be on the receiving end. Instead, my cousin, who was like my sister, got into his car and died because of the bomb I had my goons plant. She died because of the evil that I was trying to carry out. I know that Ben contracted Evelyn's murderer, John, to kill Cynthia. He didn't get the job done, but Ben's seed did. I knew I should have killed her with the rest of his family. I let Eve live and she comes back to kill my fiancé. That's what happens when you leave loose ends.

I paid for a cab to take Javier wherever he wanted to go. He was getting twisted. I didn't want him driving anywhere in that condition. He could kill an innocent person. The bartender told me that he'd make sure that Javier got inside of a cab. When I leave, I call G.

"What's going on out there son? You handling your business or should I say my business?

"Of course, Craig. Everything is going according to plan. She is hooked. She has no clue. I will say that I've enjoyed this assignment. I can't say I enjoy my current place of employment, but it's only temporary it's for a greater good, so I'll tough it out."

"Great son! I'm counting on you! You make this happen and I'll put you in a more visible position within the company. I may even throw in a new whip when you get back. "

"Word! I don't need a new whip, but I'll take it! Good looking out Pops!"

"Oh, I'm Pops now. I was Craig a few minutes ago." I say laughing.

G fills me in on some more. He tells me that she'll never see it coming. That's all that I needed to hear. This woman is going to pay. My son is going to make sure of it. *Cynthia, don't worry. I'm not going to let it go until she suffers.*

Claudia:

Living with Rochelle ain't half bad. It's like a sleep over that never ends. I haven't done any dumb or forgetful shit recently. Maybe that means that the meds are working. I thought that Rochelle would want to move her stuff into the house so that she feels more at home. She told me that all of her shit is cheap. There's no way she'd want any of that stuff in here. All she brought to the house were clothes.

"Claudia, are you ok with me having company tonight?"

"What kind of company?"

"The kind that can beat it up from the back" she says laughing.

"You old hoe. You still having one night stands at this age? Don't you think your old behind should be looking for a husband by now?"

"Look at who's talking! I don't see you with a love interest. Where's your boo?"

"I don't have a boo. I was married before you know."

"Yes, you were married for a hot second. Do you ever get any letters from the pastor, your huuuuuusband?"

"When he first got locked up, he sent me letters to make sure that I kept my mouth shut."

"I barely remember my family on some days. I doubt I'll remember enough to say something incriminating."

"Well, write it down now just in case we need to use that information on a later date.'

Rochelle was serious. She had my back. She's always had my back. Next on my list is to tell Karma that Rochelle is her biological grandmother. I can't imagine that going over well. I know she is going to be mad as hell. I also know I am going to get cussed the fuck out. I can't blame her. I'd be mad too. At least, it's only her grandmother and not her mother. I never planned on telling Ava or Karma.

Eve:

Greg didn't come into work today. He also didn't call me to tell me that he wasn't coming in. I'm not his boss, but damn, we work at the same place. Why wouldn't he tell me that he wasn't coming in. Over the weekend, things were normal. We chilled at my place. We watched movies. I cooked for him. We made love. We went to sleep. Sunday, we woke up and did it all over again. Except, on Sunday night he went home instead of staying over. We were supposed to go over his house today after work. Maybe, he is self-conscious about his place and took the day to clean it up for me.

I still haven't made it to his place. Come to think of it, I don't even know his address. He just gave me the neighborhood, but not the physical address. When I talk to him later to find out why he took the day off, I'll ask him. His phone keeps going to voice mail. He hasn't replied to my text either.

I'm getting pissed. Where is the thoughtful Greg that I know and love? Him being unreachable is fucking with me. I'm at work. I don't need to be tripping about Greg's whereabouts. I hate to turn my internal switch on *I don't give a fuck mode*, but I will. I stand up to go to the bathroom but I don't think that I can make it. Instead, I throw up inside of the wastebasket at my desk.

I am embarrassed because of the sound that came out of my mouth when I vomited. Nobody saw me, but I'm positive somebody heard me. Angel comes over to my desk to check on me. The look on her face said it all.

"What the fuck is up with you?"

"Nothing, I think I caught a bug or something." She looks at me as if she knows I'm lying.

"You caught a bug or caught some sperm Eve?"

"Damn! Could you keep your voice down in here?"

"I wasn't loud."

"Yes, you were Angel. I need you to keep this on the low."

"So, how often are you throwing up?"

"This is the first time. That's why I said I think I have a bug."

"So, you haven't been throwing up?"

"No, I've been fine."

"Ok, maybe it is a bug or it's the beginning of a long trimester of vomiting."

"I can't imagine throwing up for three months. That's torture!"

"We'll see." Angel says clearly not buying the bug excuse.

At this point, I'm worried. I aborted my other pregnancy from Mr. Uncle. I did get pregnant one more time, but that's a story I don't want to talk about. This is my first pregnancy, that I want to keep. I'm young, but old enough to take care of a child. Hopefully, Greg will feel the same way and want to build a family with me. He's going to have to do a better job of communicating in the future.

Something is up. I can feel it. Greg finally called me to swing by and then he cancelled at the last minute. When I asked him why he didn't go to work today, he said that he was having stomach problems. He stayed in the bed. He also mentioned that he didn't know that he had to check in with me. That comment wasn't appreciated. It was a bit much.

I was worried about him. He called again to say that he is going to come by later and then cancelled. He is not coming by. He said that he hoped that his stomach would feel better, but it doesn't. He just wants to chill at home. When I asked him if he wanted me to come by and take care of him, he said that he'd prefer to be alone. All that I keep thinking is that he's back peddling now. Shit. I didn't even tell him that I'm pregnant and he's already trying to shake me.

Things are, or should I say, things *were* good between us. I have no complaints. Greg has been the best boyfriend that I've ever had. I thought that I was doing my part. I always try to show him love. I give him attention. I make him feel wanted and needed. I don't nag him. *What is it that I'm doing wrong?* None of my relationships seem to work out. I need to start looking at the common denominator; me. Before I thought the issue was them, but now I'm thinking it could be me. The problem is, I don't know what it is about me that causes my relationships not to last.

Vince, Richard and now Greg? I must be giving off some type of energy or vibe that tells these dudes I'm not worth the work or a relationship. Vince cheated on me. I'm sure that he did it more than once--I know how he gets down. Knowing this, I couldn't stay with a man that steps out on me. I'd be putting my life in his hands every time we became intimate. He likes it raw. He hated when I demanded that he strap it up. Knowing him, he is probably running around town raw dogging it.

Richard was great. He worked a lot, but we had good chemistry. I got the job in Massachusetts and didn't tell him; he ended up telling me that he knew. That's what broke us up. He didn't like that "I made life decisions without him". He said that I am disrespectful. He called me a few other things too. This was something that we could have talked about but he made it into a big deal. *He* made it so that we couldn't work it out. So, I moved to Boston to start the new job. I always hoped that we'd work it out and he'd move up to Boston to be with me. His family is from Boston; I thought that alone would sweeten the pot. It didn't. Instead, he abandoned me.

I tried to start my life over in Boston. I even tried to date. Unfortunately, that was short lived. Here I am, back in Charlotte, in the same boat I left in. I am in a relationship that feels like it's good, but my gut tells me it is going to end. I didn't know guys like Greg existed in real life. It's like God gives me a taste of what a good relationship should look and feel like, then threatens to snatch it away. What the fuck did I do to deserve a life like this?

152

Didn't I pay my dues in my childhood? All I want is to be loved. All I want is a family to love. I missed out on that. Why is it I can't get that? I'm a good person. I have a good heart. I've done *one* real horrible thing, but according to God, no sin is greater than the other; right? Cynthia is gone because Craig stole my chance of having a family that loves me. I wanted him to feel what it was like to not have love. So, I killed her.

I hope he's suffering, because I'm still suffering! She was on her death bed anyway. It wasn't like she was healthy, active and living life. She was in a hospital bed because somebody shot her. She wasn't expected to wake up from her coma. When she did; Craig thought his prayers were answered, but then I fixed that.

Maybe this is happening because I still have ill will in my heart for Craig. *I don't care.* I hope he's still hurting. I hope he never gets over this. I hope he never finds love. I hope he dies a lonely motherfucker. Fuck him! And fuck Greg too. If Greg wants to act like he ain't got time for me; I won't have time for him.

***

Greg doesn't come to work on Tuesday either. Although, I am mad; I still worry about where he is and if he's ok. I'm at work battling sadness, anger and disappointment. I'm experiencing all of these emotions on top of being pregnant. I got too much pride to ask the other security guard where Greg is. Plus, I don't want him in my business. I also don't want him knowing that I don't know where my man is. As bad as I want to ask him, I don't.

Now, I'm tripping. The entire work week has gone by and Greg just disappeared. I don't know if he took sick days or vacation days. I haven't asked anyone about him because I want to avoid being asked about him. I don't know what I'll say. The more days go by, the more he is showing me that he could care less about me. That has become disturbingly obvious but I don't want everyone else at work to know that. I need to call my sister. Karma answers on the first ring.

"I don't know where he is."

"Who are you referring to and what happened to "hello"? Where are your manners?"

"Hello Karma, I can't find my boyfriend."

"Mmmmmm. Did you stop by his house?"

"No"

"Why the hell not?"

"Because I never got the address to where he lives."

"You've got to be kidding me."

"What? I was supposed to go over to his house Monday but…"

"But what? He cancelled on you or did he lie and say he was sick?"

"He said he was sick and didn't come to work that day."

"I hate to break it to you, but if you don't know your man's address *and* you've never been inside his home; he's not your boyfriend."

"Karma, I'm not trying to hear that bullshit right now. I didn't call you for that. I'm worried. He hasn't been to work in a week and hasn't called."

"So, why don't you ask someone at work about him. Oh, never mind, you're trying to save face. You don't want them to know that you don't know."

"Exactly. Karma I was going to tell him about the baby last Monday. I never got the chance. I need to know what happened to him. I need to know if he's ok. None of it makes sense. Things were good between us. As a matter of fact, things were great. I think something bad has happened to him. Oh, my God! Karma, what if something bad happened to him. Maybe I should call the police."

"Girl please. This ain't nothing that you need to call the police for. I'll find out what happened to him. Tell me everything you know about him."

I tell Karma everything that Greg's ever told me. I don't know if what I am telling her is fact or fiction but I know that she'll find out what's going on with him. She has just as good, if not better, of an investigative mind as I do. And, she's not going to be clouded by pregnancy or emotions. Right now, I'm just not up for the hassle. Any other time, I'd be game. This time it's different. The fact is I don't want to find out that he's just another bad choice that I can add to my lengthy list of bad choices. This is why she has to do this instead of me.

Craig:

G came back sooner than I expected. He told me not to worry. He did his job. Now, I need to let "time" do its job. It is a done deal. G made her feel what love is supposed to feel like.

He made her let her guard down. I hope she was making plans for a future with him. I bet she finally thought that she found 'the one'. He made her vulnerable. He made her believe in love. Then--he left her.

She didn't have a chance to say goodbye; just like I didn't get a chance to tell Cynthia goodbye. He left her with unanswered questions. Did Eve think that I wouldn't have questions to ask Cynthia? G left her worrying about him. I hope she worries herself sick. All I did was worry about Cynthia while she was in the hospital. G left her feeling powerless. That is exactly how I felt with Cynthia's situation.

I still think about that night that I proposed to Cynthia. I went all out. I paid to have John Legend sing her favorite song to her in our hotel suite. The way that she looked at me when she saw what I'd done for her...

Never again will I find a woman like Cynthia. That was my second chance at love. My first chance was with Evelyn; I let her slip right out of my hands. When she went off to college I didn't fight for her. I let her go. And till this day, I regret that. Decades later, Charlene's offspring--named after my first love--snatched Cynthia away from me. It's ironic that these two women have the same name. One I love and the other I hate.

When she finds out that G is my son, she'll understand the lengths I'll go to retaliate. Killing her would have been easy. She hurt my heart. No--she took my heart. And because of that I'm going to smash hers. I'll have her thinking that she's not worthy of a good man. I'll have her questioning if she'll ever meet a man that truly loves her. Her self-esteem will be so much at rock bottom, she'll torture herself. I won't have to.

Joan:

I never would have guessed that what seemed like one of the worst days I've had would end on a good note. The patron that pulled Jonathan off of me, knows me. He went to school with me. He knows that I was once Jonathan and that I transitioned to Joan. He knows and he still treats me like a human being instead of a freak.

We took a walk to my car after the Jonathan fiasco. He asked to see me again. It caught me off guard. I wasn't expecting him to want to see me again. I was pleased to be able to just have a conversation with an attractive man and not worry about if he knows I'm transgender. He came over the next night. When he was over we *just* talked. We talked about folks that we knew in high school and what they are doing now. The conversation was easy. It was natural. It felt too good to be true. I thought that he might be feeling me, but I talked myself out of that. That would *really* make this too good to be true. We have been spending time with each other for weeks now. Maybe he wants to be more than friends. The sound of my phone ringing interrupts my thoughts. *Who is calling me at this hour in the morning?*

"Hello" I say smiling after I see the caller id.

"Joan?" His raspy voice sounds good to my ears.

"Yes, this is she." I'm grinning hard.

"This is the man that has no idea what it is like to date a transgender woman, but would like to take that chance if you are willing to take the chance with me."

"Huh?"

"I want to date you Joan. I've known you since the ninth grade. I've seen you. *I know you*. I knew your mom. She was a very kind woman. Did you know that when it snowed, I used to come to your house and shovel your mom's car out? I shoveled the driveway, the walkway and the steps. Your mom used to pay me good money."

"That was you all bundled up like it was twenty below out there?"

"Yes and you're welcome" he says laughing.

"What? Do I owe you a thank you?"

"Yes, you do Joan. I protected you from the elements. You never had to go outside and shovel. You should thank me for that."

"So, I owe you huh?"

"No. You don't owe me Joan. It was a pleasure to help your mom out. I can't believe that you didn't know that it was me out there. I did all of that before school. You and I were in the same home room for four years. You acted like I didn't exist."

"Oh, is that what you thought I was doing? You thought that I was ignoring you."

"That's what it felt like" he says softly.

"I spent my last year at school trying not to bring attention to myself. That's pretty hard to do while you're transitioning. I wasn't ignoring anyone. I hoped that folks ignored me."

"I think that you are beautiful Joan."

"Thank you David. You aren't too bad yourself."

"Not just on the outside; your heart is beautiful. I sense that you haven't been told that enough. God put me into your life to remind you of your beauty. Never shrink for anyone Joan. You deserve to be respected, loved, protected and happy. You deserve to be yourself. You deserve some peace instead of chaos. I'm going to be that man to add to your life instead of the one that subtracts. I'm here to support you and build you up when you feel like you've been knocked down. If things don't work out between us romantically, at least we will have built a solid friendship. I doubt that we will ever know. Do you believe in love at first sight?"

"Yes, but you and I've have seen each other before. That's not love at first sight."

"I believe in love at each sight. Each time I see you, I see love."

Did he just say love? "Love?"

"Yes love. I know that I will love you one day. My heart whispered it to me already. If you listen to your heart, you'll hear that love is inevitable between us. Don't let the short time span we've been reconnecting fool you. I've known you since ninth grade. I probably know just as much about you as your best friend. All of these late-night phone calls we've been having has caught me up on what I missed. Joan, give us a chance. Give love a chance. Are you ready?"

I'm scared. God, please don't play with me. "Yes, David, I'm ready."

BJ:

Vi has been working late for the last week or so. I know she doesn't want me to worry about her, but I can't help it. She typically doesn't work this late –this often. However, she tells me she can't predict if she'll have a late customer. Lately, it's been one every night. What's worse is she hasn't been sleeping here – she's been going back to her place. So, I tell her to call me once she settles in. On the first night, she did; yet, that was the only time she did. Now she just calls me in the morning.

I miss her body in my bed at night. After I finish work, I have nothing to look forward to. I have no one to cook for. I'm bored. Victoria acts like she has no time for me. She told me that she'll come see me on Sunday but she won't be staying the night because she has a football party to go to. She didn't even ask if I wanted to go. Still, I don't let it bother me. I'm looking forward to spending a lazy Sunday with my boo.

I'm making spaghetti when the phone rings. I hear it, but I can't get to it because I'm draining the spaghetti. I'll see who it is after I wash the pasta off. *Whoever it is will leave a message.* When I check my phone, I see Victoria left a message.

"Hey, I wanted to let you know that I am going to be late. I have a few errands that I need to run before I come by. I'll see you around two o'clock. Hope you cooked. I'll be starving by then."

At least she gave me the courtesy of letting me know that she'll be late. I can't stand it when someone knows that they are running late and they wait until the time that they are supposed to show up to call. Karma used to do that with me. It made me feel like I was an afterthought. I'm so glad that I'm not dealing with her anymore. Vi is nothing like her. That's exactly what I need.

Ever since that night that I smelled Karma's brand of perfume on Vi, I've been thinking more about Karma. I haven't been thinking about her like I used to; just every now and then she

160

pops on my mind. It's usually something erotic. To shake my thoughts of her, I have to think about the fucked-up things she's done or said to me. Karma had such a hold on me. I would have done anything for her. Yet, she doesn't deserve me. Taking a sip of wine, I doze off thinking about Karma compared to Vi.

Buuuuuuuuuuuuuuuuuuzz!

Damn! Who the hell is ringing the bell like they don't have any sense. It couldn't be Vi. She has a key. *Wait.* She told me that she misplaced them a few days ago. *Is it two o'clock already?* As I walk to the buzzer, I look at my watch. It's almost four o'clock. I open the door; it's Vi. Although, I was asleep and unaware of the time, I still put on a sour face.

"You're late."

"I know" she says as she walks in. She continues, "I got caught up."

"You have me waiting on you for hours and all you can say is that you got caught up."

"Girl please. You act like you were up worrying about me. Your ass was asleep. You got sleep lines on your face. I can leave if you don't want to spend any time with me. I'm sure I can find something else to do until it's time to head over to the football party."

Something about her response feels so familiar. Karma would say some shit like that to me. She is the master of flipping shit. She reminds you that she doesn't need you. Then you feel like shit when you realize that you're the needy one. What sucks more than that is that you find yourself seeking the person that treats you beneath your worth. This woman had me doing things that I knew wasn't right. She had me acting out of character. All I wanted to do was please her.

"Stop tripping. You ain't going anywhere. I cooked this meal for you. We are going to sit down and have a nice dinner and catch up. What's the gossip at the shop? Meet any interesting customers? Any weird tattoo requests?"

That broke the ice. The entire time we talk about her. She never asks me how I was doing or even what I did while we were apart. I am starting to think that Vi is selfish. She only thinks about what is going on in her world."

"Did you change your perfume? *There's that smell again.*

"No, why do you ask?"

"Oh, because I smelled it on you a few weeks back."

"You know I'm always up close and personal with my clients. You probably smell their perfume. Why? You like it?'

"It's ok, but did you go to work today? Why would I smell someone else's perfume on you?"

"Do I have to tell you every move that I make BJ? Please don't suffocate me."

"Suffocate you! I haven't seen you in a week. You don't come here after work. We hardly talk on the phone. You seem real busy lately. Business must be booming."

"Look Bitch! You're getting out of hand. We've only known each other for a hot little minute and you act like we're married. This is getting to be too much for me. You are too intense for me. I'm not sure where all this is coming from but I'm thinking maybe I should fall back. Dinner looks delicious by the way. Too bad I lost my appetite."

Did she just refer to me as a bitch? I'm so tired of women thinking they can treat me any kind of way.

"Take your raggedy, low budget, tattooing ass out of my place. I'm nobody's bitch and I'm way too good for you. Take what shit you have here and get the hell out!

She says nothing. With a sinister smile spread across her face, she gets her shit than throws the keys that she said she lost at me and leaves. If I didn't know any better, I'd think she was related to Karma. I think I'm going to chill for a while. The dating scene is really testing my nerves.

It's like she smelled blood. Ten minutes after Vi leaves, Karma calls my phone. I told myself that I wasn't going to answer her calls, but I did anyway.

"You miss me yet?"

"Yup. Come over."

"I'm downstairs." I smile. Karma is such a dude. I buzz her in.

When she comes in, she kisses me on my cheek. I lock the door after she enters. With the last lock, she pushes me against my door and tongue kisses me. She puts her hand inside of my panties and I am immediately ready to head to the bedroom. Though, if I know Karma, I know we won't make it to the bedroom. At this point, I could care less.

I've missed her touch. I've missed her smell. I've missed how she tastes. I surrender to Karma. She has me under her spell. She bites my nipple through my jersey fitted shirt. Her left hand is just as skillful as her right. She is ambidextrous. While her left hand is working inside of me, Karma pulls my shirt and bra up at the same time.

163

She licks my nipples and then softly bites them. I'm so turned on by what she's doing to me, my knees feel like they are going to give. I'm pinned against my door. For a quick second, I get a moment of clarity and I almost tell Karma to stop, but then she removes her hand and replaces it with her mouth. There's no turning back now. I cry as I orgasm. Karma looks at me as if I'm pathetic.

This will be my last time dealing with Karma. I see it in her eyes. She's disgusted. I know she just wanted sex without any emotions. I made it more than that when I started crying. But I couldn't help it. My girlfriend broke up with me twenty minutes ago and I already have Karma's hand down my pants. I never fully got over Karma. If I had, she wouldn't be here looking at me like I have issues. I look at her and say "What?"

"I was hoping that I was wrong about you BJ. You proved me right. You should talk to someone about your emotions. If you let your emotions control you, you'll always get hurt. You need to know when to turn them off. You knew what was up when you let me in. I came for sex. I didn't come for love or love making. Sadly, you can't handle that. I thought maybe we could be friends, but that's not gonna happen. Your feelings are too strong for me for us to be just friends. I can't have you hating on me whenever I meet someone new. I don't need that type of friendship."

Buuuuuuuuuuuuuuuuuuuuuuzz!

We both hear the buzzer. I quickly straighten my clothes and wipe my eyes. I'm not sure who it is. I'm not expecting anyone, but anything is better than dealing with what Karma is telling me right now. I buzz them in without asking who it is.

"You and I are no more. I just want to make sure we are clear. When I leave, forget you ever knew me. Because, believe me--you are already forgotten." Karma says with a mean look on her face.

I open the door to see who it is that rang the buzzer. It's Vi. I smile. She wants to make up. I know it. I can't wait to see the look on Karma's face when she sees Vi. I turn around and address Karma.

"Karma, believe me. You don't have to worry. You are also already forgotten."

Vi walks in. She walks right past me and puts my parking garage pass on the table. I guess she forgot to leave it. *Shit.* She's not here to make up. I look at Karma and see that she has this smirk on her face. *What the fuck is up with her?*

"Oh, so this is your girlfriend huh?" Karma says, still with a smirk. Its smug. I don't like it at all. I'm ready to slap the smirk right off of her face. Vi answers for me.

"Ex-girlfriend. She thought I was her wife." *Did this Bitch just put our business in the streets?*

"Small world." Karma says still smiling. Within seconds, Karma is tongue kissing my girlfriend. I'm beyond shocked. I can't move. I don't know what to do. Karma has her hands all over Vi and she's letting her. These two bitches are disrespectful. They obviously know each other. I guess that answers why I smelled Karma's brand of perfume on her. It was Karma that I was smelling. I scream.

"GET THE FUCK OUT OF MY HOUSE!"

"Put me the fuck out." Karma says and then looks at me as if she's ready to beat my ass. She's the one who is in the wrong. In *my* house tongue kissing *my* girlfriend. She's fucking crazy. Vi—Tori—*Victoria*--whatever the hell her name is, says nothing. She got too many damn names for me. I know she's waiting to see what happens next. I guess I'm going to have to beat Karma's ass. Did she forget that I helped her sister Eve when she was getting jumped on that African boat cruise? She must have. Nonetheless, she's about to find out who she's dealing with.

Karma:

Tori sees BJ and I going at it like two girls in middle school. She pulls us apart and then takes my spot. She is beating BJ down like she stole something. I let her. The only way BJ is going to get over me, is if she hates me. So, I stand back like a boss and let my goon get at her.

Tori beats her so badly that she is now unconscious. Moments later, she tells me to sit tight while she runs to her car to get something. While she runs out, I make sure that BJ is still breathing. She is. She just got knocked the fuck out. When Tori comes back in, her work bag is in hand. Damn, I may have met someone that's as crazy as me.

We tie BJ up just in case she wakes up from the pain. Tori spreads her legs open, then starts to take out her tools.

"What are you going to write?" I ask as she starts prepping BJ's inner thigh.

"It's going to say "I suck dick".

We look at each other and laughter erupts!

"No don't do that to the girl. That would be fucked up."

"Why not? She *stays* on our dick." *Damn, Tori sure has an evil side to her.*

"True, but that's hitting her below the belt."

"Well, what do you want me to write? I can't stand clingy bitches."

"That's it! I can't have you writing lies on the girl, but you can definitely write that."

"Write what?"

After I tell her, Tori kneels down on the floor next to BJ and starts going in. Tori effortlessly writes what she is told. When she's done, a huge grin spreads across her face. She is pleased with her artwork. She didn't take long at all. Tori has skills.

In big, bold, red cursive letters— on BJ's inner thigh it reads "*Watch out!*". On the right thigh, in red ink it reads "*I'm Clingy!*".

When BJ wakes up and finds out what we did, she's going to be mad as hell. I'm not afraid of BJ reporting this to the police--that's not how she rolls. However, we may have to watch our backs for a minute.

About a month has passed and neither one of us have heard from BJ. Yet, it looks like I traded in one stalker for another. Tori has been sweating me since we beat BJ's ass. *Might have to get rid of her too.*

***

My grandmother has been declining since our last dinner a few weeks ago. She calls me today and tells me that she is not my grandmother. I ignore her crazy forgetful ass. This is the same woman that attended my mother's funeral then asks me where my mother is. Now, *all of a sudden,* she doesn't know that I'm her granddaughter. I know I should be more understanding, but she is really irritating me with this dementia madness. Is she supposed to get a pass due to her dementia every time that she hurts my feelings? When she invited me over for dinner again, I told her no. I don't need to see that craziness up close and personal.

The more I think of her, the more I miss my mother. I miss my mother so much; I dream about her. Every time I go to the gym, I think about her. She was big on making sure I kept my figure right. I know she wanted to see me get married and have children. Maybe it's best that she is not here. I'd hate for her to be disappointed in me.

I've aborted a child and I am in no hurry to get married. At this point, I can't see any man that will sign off on my explicit sexual behaviors while being married. I may need to go to some place where polygamy is legal. I'm going to have to get all this out of my system, before I even think about marriage or children. I can't expose a child to this life I'm living.

Speaking of children, Eve is as serious as a heart attack. She isn't getting rid of her child. She's going to carry her fake name using, no picture taking, no social media having, missing boyfriend's child. I got to give it to him, Greg covered his tracks. He made sure that the job wasn't going to release any of his information, by filing a false grievance against Eve.

Eve is so afraid; she thought that she was going to lose her job and her benefits. Any other time, she wouldn't care, but this pregnancy got her thinking for two. She isn't showing yet so the job doesn't know. And she's not going to tell them until she's out of her first trimester.

Long story short, they aren't going to fire her. Unfortunately, now she has a blemish on her work history with the company. I told her to fight it. I know damn well she wasn't stalking Greg. He did that to keep her from getting to his information. I got to give it to him. That was a good move. If I didn't know any better, I'd think we were in the same family. Although I've never met him, he intrigues me.

I've been staying at the condo laying low because I thought that BJ was going to try to do something crazy. Here, I have a door man; so, if she happens to find her way over here, at least I have a buffer. My condo fee pays his salary. I slipped him a few hundred on the side to be extra vigilant. He needs to make sure nobody is in here who isn't supposed to be. I even showed him her picture; I showed him Tori's too. I didn't want her crazy behind up here either seeking me out.

Staying at the condo is cool and all, but it's not home. It's missing an importance piece. My mother's presence. Although she's gone. I can still feel her when I'm at the house. Because of that, I will never sell the family home. I decide to head back to the house. As I'm pulling up, I start to contemplate going back to the condo. Rochelle's car is in the driveway. *I know that my grandmother is giving her good money; you'd think that she'd upgrade her whip.* Although it is Rochelle's car, I know she isn't here alone.

I guess my grandmother is here because I've been avoiding her. She makes me uneasy. You never know what is going to come out of her mouth. Before, she was predictable. You could count on some foul shit coming out of her mouth. It's different now—especially when she asks about my mother. Every once and a while she'll ask" how my no-good daddy is doing". She forgets that he'd dead too. I lost both of my parents and now I'm losing my grandmother; except, she is still living.

169

It's early. I've noticed that she is more coherent in the day time. Once the sun starts going down, her memory gets worse. I know I said that she needs to be at the house with me, but I'm glad she has Rochelle. I don't think I could handle her. She drains me emotionally. Physically, I'm sure that I could take care of her. I'm just not in the right mental space to take her on. They are both in the kitchen sipping on mint tea when I walk in.

"Been out hoeing again?" *I guess she's in her right mind.*

"Well Good Morning to you too!" I sarcastically say.

"Hi Karma. Your grandmother and I wanted to talk to you. We've been having breakfast here every day for the last two weeks hoping that we'd run into you." Rochelle explains.

"Couldn't my grandmother just call me?"

"You little disrespectful snot, don't talk about me like I'm not here."

"Sometimes, I wonder Claudia." She's not going to like that I called her Claudia.

"You grown now? You think you can call me Claudia? We aren't equals. You're a kid!"

"Hey you two! We are here for a reason. Let's not waste time on this negativity."

"Why are you two here? What is so important? It's not like my grandmother will remember what you want to talk to me about today. A phone call would have sufficed."

"Isn't she an evil witch Rochelle?" My grandmother mean mugs me.

"Karma, I'm here to facilitate and to answer any questions that you may have for me. There's one more person that needs to be a part of this discussion. That person will be here shortly. Why don't you grab some tea or hot chocolate while we wait?"

"Rochelle, this is my house. I don't need you offering me my own shit. I'm going to pass on the hot beverage and get something a little stronger. Something tells me I'm going to need it."

The doorbell rings.

"I'll get it." I say. I go to the door and look through the oval brushed glass in the middle. There's an older man; and he's white.

"Hello Beautiful!" The elderly white man greets me.

"Hi. Can I help you?"

"Yes. I'm here to see Claudia."

"Oh, Ok. I guess you are the missing piece to this awful puzzle."

"I guess I am." He says smiling with his perfect teeth. He obviously takes pride in his appearance. The teeth smiling at me aren't dentures. They are real. *He must have a good dental plan.*

"Bring your white ass in the kitchen Alvin." My grandmother yells.

"Coming Dear!" He says laughing and shaking his head.

The joke is on me. I have no idea what is going on or who this white man is that obviously knows my grandmother. I've never seen him before in my life. Maybe she knows him from her former life as a First Lady. It's hard to imagine my grandmother as the First Lady of a church. She really fooled them. Don't get me wrong; she believes in God, but she's no saint.

I know that I have never seen this Alvin guy in my life. I don't forget faces. Yet, there's something about him that has me second guessing if I forgot his face and we've met before. As I search the files of my brain, I take a good look at him again. This time he has his glasses off. Then it hits me. It's his eyes. His eyes are like my mother's. They are creamy caramel brown. They are like my eyes. This man is family. I don't know how, but he *definitely* is.

Eve:

Is God punishing me? Is this because I killed Cynthia. Does God not think I'm worth shit? Doesn't my childhood count for *something*? I was raised by a drug addict. I find out that my drug addict mother really isn't my mother. My best friend messes with my ex-boyfriend, Vince. Richard, my upgrade, is really a down grade and he turns out to be a jerk that I fell in love with. He abandons me when I move to Massachusetts for a job. My biological parents were killed by my sister's uncle; the sister I never knew I had. I learned that Ben was my dad after I investigated him for a case at my old job. I learned this after I let him taste me. I'm grossed out just thinking about that. I try my best to shake that image. It's sick.

Then I move back to Charlotte and work things out with Gina. I get a job. I meet a man at work. We form a great relationship and then he ups and leaves before I get a chance to tell him that I'm pregnant with his child. I am having a child by a man and I don't even know his real name. My life couldn't be any more tragic. There's no room for it.

I just don't know what to do anymore. I'd say that I have nothing to live for if I didn't have a life growing inside of me. I'm so sad. I'm sad every day. The only thing that brings me joy is his baby. I didn't sign up to be a single mom--I signed up for love. I would have killed myself trying to find out what I did that scared Greg away. Why would he file a grievance against me? Why would he leave without telling me anything? *Where is he?*

It's like he never existed. Nobody at work talks about him. I can't openly ask about him due to the grievance he filed against me. Everybody at work is tight lipped. I tried to ask Joe, the older security guard, about him. He looked at me and said "Greg who?" I knew that it was a lost cause after I found out that they got to Joe. If he isn't talking, nobody is.

Angel tried to help me out, but even her connects weren't talking. I figured that at least one person would give up some information. I know every employee doesn't have loyalty. I just have to find the right one to talk. As I'm racking my brain, I get an idea. I have to be a little shady to through with it, this idea might actually work. At this point, I'm desperate. Karma told me to be patient. She promised to get some information, but she's not working quickly enough for me.

The video footage of Helen may be the answer to getting answers. I decide to play my hand. I don't know how this is going to go but it's my last shot at finding out anything about Greg.

"Good Morning Helen" I say with a fake smile on my face. She doesn't respond.

"Helen, did you hear me? I said good morning to you."

"And."

"*And?* When someone greets you, you greet them back."

"Look. What do you want? You know that I don't like you. There's no reason for me to act like you and I are good when we're not."

"I was trying to be civil, but since you can't be, I'll stop."

"I have work to do. Get to the point."

"I was wondering if you might happen to know any information about Greg."

"Yes, I do."

"What a relief! What do you know?"

"What a relief? You think I'm giving up any info. I'm not telling you anything."

"Why do you have to be so hateful Helen?"

"You started this shit. You think that I'm going to help you after you tried to hurt me?"

"No, I believe *you* are the one that started this. You've hated on me since I started working here. It's like you perceived me as a threat. I'm just trying to get my check and go home. Instead, you treated me like I was trying to take your check."

"Listen, I don't have time for this. Unlike you, I have work to do."

Time to play my hand. "What kind of work do you 'have to do' Helen? Do you mean the kind of work that you do after hours selling your oral skills? Have you sucked every dick in this company? I'll give it to you. You are getting paper. Your customers are *definitely* satisfied because you have several repeat customers. You've got to be making more than what you make here. I admire your hustler's spirit, but I don't think that the company would share my admiration. So, if you want to keep your job and your hustle, you're gonna want to tell me all that you know about Greg."

I knew that footage would come in handy. Helen didn't have much info, but what she did know is where he lived. Little did I know; she gave him a ride home one day. There's no doubt in my mind that she was trying to add him to the roster. She gave me the address. I am going there during lunch. If I could go now, I would.

I got five more minutes before my lunch break. The desk phone rings and I recognize the number. I send that shit to voicemail. That client will have me on the phone for an hour. *Not today buddy.* The phone rings again and it's the same number. The number disappears after one ring because I have my phone on send calls. I'm now staring at the digital clock on my phone. Only one minute has passed. Five minutes' feels like forever when you're waiting on it.

Finally, it's lunch time. I grab my keys and his address and hustle down the corridor. As I walk towards the elevator, Helen is coming out of the bathroom. She is walking towards me, but she's ignoring me. Once she gets close, she gives me a dirty ass look. I'm sure she would love to beat my ass if she thought she could. But she doesn't try me. *She ain't stupid.* Passing her by, I roll my eyes. I don't blame her for being mad. I threatened her income; I'd be mad at me too.

I'm in my car listening to "Moment in Life" an old-school jam, by Nikki Minaj. I love this song. It is so motivating. My favorite part comes on that I know word for word. For a short moment, I'm feeling extremely confident. Yet, as I start to rap along with Nikki, my nerves act up.

I don't know what I'm going to say when I get to Greg's house. I try not to think about it too hard but I can't shake it. I'm hurt. My hormones are messing with me. I'm mad. I'm sad. I'm worried about him. I feel bad for myself. Emotionally, I'm just all over the place. A lump starts to form in my throat. I'm about to cry. I try to keep it in, but I'm overwhelmed. The tears start flowing. I'm crying. No. I'm not crying--I'm sobbing. *I'm a wreck.* I can hardly see. I keep wiping my eyes forgetting I don't wear waterproof mascara. Now there's mascara all over my hand. That's what I get for trying to substitute my hand as a napkin. I taste salt on my upper lip only to realize it's snot.

I can't go see him looking like a crazy person. I look a hot mess. I need to get it together so I pull over. According to the navigational system, I'm a block away from his place. Looking into my visor mirror I see I look worse than I thought. I grab my spare make-up bag in the glove compartment. Thank God I have make up wipes. I wipe all of what's left of my eye make-up off. I look at myself in the mirror. I'm bare. I'm vulnerable. I'm open.

Once I drive up to his place. I wait a few minutes to allow the redness of my eyes to fade. I don't have any extra mascara or eyeliner in my make-up bag. I do have lipstick and lip gloss though, so, I put some on. I make a mental note to put some spare mascara and eyeliner in my car for next time. I look at myself one last time. I'm ready.

Claudia:

"Alvin sit down." He does as he's told.

"Hello Rochelle. Always a pleasure." He greets waiting for a response.

"Mmmmmm" Rochelle forcefully responds.

"Don't y'all start. I have y'all here for an important conversation. This is a conversation that I should have had with my daughter; I don't want to miss the opportunity to talk to my granddaughter."

"Are you going somewhere?" Karma sarcastically asks.

"Look, Karma, I'm gonna need you to show some respect. What I have to talk to you about won't be a comfortable conversation; however, I'm gonna need you to be patient and hear me out. You can't go stomping out like a child because you're mad. I need you to just sit here and listen. You can ask whatever you want when we are done. I shouldn't take too long. Do we have an agreement?'

"I guess." Karma answers.

"Well, you know I don't like to sugar coat anything. Me and Rochelle slept with the same man. The white man that is sitting beside you is who we slept with."

"What do I care if you and Rochelle like to share men?"

"Karma, I know I told you that I didn't want you to talk until I was finished. When I am finished, you can talk all the shit you want. Right now, I need to focus on getting this out while

177

I'm still clear. When shit starts to get fuzzy, good luck to you if you think you're going to get some answers."

"Continue."

"Rochelle and I slept with the same man, but I was in a relationship with him. I was stupid enough to think he'd leave his fiancé for me. I wasn't as smart as I thought I was. I got pregnant. Rochelle slept with him too, and ended up pregnant. We were in the hospital at the same time and had our baby girls a day a part."

"I didn't know you had a daughter Rochelle. Where is she at?" Karma interrupts.

"Should I answer it or should you Claudia?" Rochelle asks. She looks worried.

"I'll answer her. Karma, Ava was Rochelle's daughter."

Karma looks confused.

"Ava was my daughter. I raised her, but Rochelle is her biological mother. I lost my daughter after the delivery. My best friend was having a baby by a man she didn't love. Even though, she knew that I loved him. Rochelle wasn't ready for a child but she also didn't want to abort her child. So, she signed your momma over to me the day that she was born."

"Alvin, your dumb ass would have known this, had you shown any interest or better yet, compassion." He says nothing. I turn my attention back to Karma.

"Karma, Ava never knew. I never told her."

"What the fuck am I supposed to say?" Karma blurts out.

178

"You don't have to say shit. I didn't want to lose what is left of my mind before getting the chance to tell you" I snap back.

"So, do you feel *good* now that you gotten it off your chest? I mean really… You couldn't just die and leave it in a letter for me to read? Most people would do that. What good does that information serve me? So, I'm supposed to start referring to Rochelle as my grandmother now? You really know how to fuck up someone's day *Claudia*. Rochelle's my grandmother. So, that makes you, who? Nobody. Right?"

"You sure are an ignorant heifer. Be grateful that I told you. You still have the opportunity to decide if you want to ask questions or not. If I was dead and gone, who would you ask? *Your Mama?"* I feel bad as soon as I say it.

Karma storms out of the kitchen and then re-enters. "Fuck you." She says before leaving again.

"Karma!" Alvin calls out to her. I roll my eyes. *Did he really think that she'd come back for him? Serves him right. He never came back for me.*

She doesn't come back. She doesn't come out of her room for the rest of the night. Alvin told me that he will be sure to stay in touch and to make himself available if she has any questions about his side of the family. For some reason, I don't believe him.

Rochelle said nothing the entire time. She didn't feel like it was her place. After a couple hours, she and I head back to our place. On the way home, Rochelle asks if I want her to reach out to Karma on her own. I tell her no.

That set up may have been too overwhelming for all parties involved. Maybe I should have just met with Karma one-on-one first. Then we could have had a conversation on a later date with the rest of them if she had questions. I just feel like I'm in a race against time. I don't know how long I'll be in my right mind. It scares and saddens me.

It's almost like I'm planning for my death. Who wants to do that? Nobody. What do I have to look forward to? A life of confusion is what the next phase is for me. I can't believe that I'm going out like this. Maybe, I'll get lucky and catch a terminal illness. That way I'll die quickly and without fear, because I won't remember shit. Knowing my luck, I'll live to be one hundred.

Karma:

So, I met my grandfather today. I always trust my gut. I knew his eyes looked familiar. I knew that he was family but I didn't expect him to be *my mother's* father. She told me that she never knew her dad. I'm upset that my mother wasn't at the table with me. We were supposed to find this out together, as a family. No. She was supposed to find this out first. Instead, my fraud of a grandmother unloaded her sins upon me. Rochelle and my grandmother were both fucking the same man--at the same time. They both knew that he already had a girlfriend and didn't care. I guess, messy shit just runs in my family.

I need some time to process this. I assume that my grandmother gave Alvin my phone number because he just called me. I told him no disrespect is intended, but I'm not ready to talk to him. I'm not sure when I will be ready to talk. I hope that he doesn't expect me to start calling him Grandpa. I also hope Claudia doesn't think that I'm just going to latch on to the idea of having new family. If she thinks I'm going to embrace Grandpa Alvin with open arms; she's bugging. He missed my whole life. The times that I needed a grandfather have come and gone. I'm not looking for any new family.

My grandmother texts me; she knows that I won't answer if she calls. She also knows that I am too nosey not to check the text. I look down at my phone and read.

'DON'T LET YOUR EMOTIONS DO YOUR THINKING FOR YOU.' That's it. No hint of an apology anywhere to be found. I'm thinking that she would write more since I figure that she is a slow texter. I wait. Nope. Nothing. That's all that she texts.

CRASH!

What the ...

I run to my bedroom window which faces the front yard. I look outside and see my window shield smashed. I can't tell what it is that did the damage but I'm assuming it's a brick. My car alarm is going off and it has started to rain. *Fuck*, my interior is going to get wet. Standing in front of my car--is BJ. I'm on the phone dialing my car insurance company. They need to get someone to fix my window by tomorrow morning. I'm pissed. I have other cars, but that was my mother's car. I know that Ava's looking down on me demanding that I fuck BJ up for that.

She doesn't run away. BJ just stands there. It looks like she is crying. Her eye make-up is smudged; black mascara is running down her face as if she's crying black tears. Her hair is getting drenched by the rain, but she doesn't move. She just stands there and stares up at my window. Not yelling or talking crazy--just standing there looking crazy. I stick my middle finger up at her.

You'd think that by now she'd know who she is dealing with. That's some risky behavior she's exhibiting. She's lucky I'm going to let this one slide. She's clearly lost an important marble. I head outside to move my car into the garage. The only reason why it wasn't in the garage is because my grandmother's bestie parked in front of it. I couldn't comfortably pull in.

BJ got her ass beat and lost two women on the same day. I guess she was still mad. I don't blame her. If I was her, I'd be mad if I couldn't have me too. By the time that I get outside, she's gone. I open the car door and I see the culprit. I was right. It is a brick. But it's not an ordinary brick. This brick has tattoo needles wrapped around it with a chain. There's glass all over my seat and my floor. I will have to clean it enough to sit in the car. Realizing, I'm out in this rain a lot longer than I want to be, I go and grab my mini hand held vacuum cleaner from the trunk to get started. Although it takes a little while, the driver's seat is now clean. I pull my car into the garage then text Tori. She's going to need some new needles in the morning if she plans on working.

BJ didn't lose all her marbles. She had enough sense to be gone by the time I made it outside. If she was still there--when I got there--that would have confirmed her mental status for me. My mother not only made sure that I knew how to take care of a man; she also made sure that I knew how to take care of myself in case another woman tried me. I still remember the day she told me I'd be taking self-defense courses.

"Karma, pretty girls just can't be pretty. They have to be tough. Growing up, I got hated on because of my beauty. I got in plenty of fights with ugly girls. They were insecure. All of the fights weren't fair fights. I've gotten jumped by a group of girls more than once. I don't ever want you to be at a disadvantage. You are going to have to learn how to beat a bitch's ass down. More importantly, you are going to need to learn how to get a man up off of you if he tries to take something without your permission. Being beautiful can be a blessing and a curse."

Eve:

He's gone! He up and moved without saying anything to me! No note! NO NOTHING! I cry like someone has died. *Someone has died.* The Eve that believed there was a chance of finally having love was murdered today. She's gone. The Eve that resurrected understands that life owes her nothing. Life is cruel. It isn't fair. Life hurts.

As I sit in the car feeling sorry for myself and angry at the world, I notice something brownish red on my seat. I didn't notice it there before. I scoot my butt back to see what's on the seat and press my index finger into the stain. It's still wet. I feel my chest getting tight. It's getting hard for me to breathe. This has happened before. I'm about to have an anxiety attack. I try to calm myself down. I can't. It feels like the space in the car is getting smaller. *Devil just take me!*

Karma:

Eve hasn't bugged me for any information lately. She was calling every day but I told her that I would hit her up once I had useful information. I got some useful information now. Shit is always so messy with this family. I found out who her man is and where he is. I thought about going to his place and paying him a visit, but then I decided to go somewhere else.

"Hey Uncle Craig"

"Karma! What you doing out this way?"

"I figured I'd come to the source."

"Oh, Ok. You want something huh? You need some intel or something?" He laughs.

"Yup. I'll tell you what I know. All I need from you is to answer why."

"You got that. Let me hear what you think you know."

"You sent G to North Carolina to get inside of Eve's head. You strategically went for the heart. You went for the emotional kill instead of just killing her. That's twice that you let her live. Why?"

"Good assessment Young Ava." I wait for him to continue.

"Does G even know who she is?"

"I told him that she and her daddy both played a part in Cynthia's death."

"So, he doesn't know who she is. I know G. He's your son, but he doesn't have that switch to shut down his compassion at the drop of a dime, like you do. G wouldn't have been able to do this if he knew who she was and what she's gone through. He would have passed on this assignment. You know that too. That's why you didn't tell him."

"I didn't tell him because he didn't need to know. His loyalty lies with me; with family. Where's your loyalty lie Karma? I know that you figured out that it was Eve that killed Cynthia. You didn't tell me. I had a hunch that you knew something. That's why I had your text history, voice messages pulled. I was shocked when I saw that message. I was even more shocked when I found out who it was that you texted. You let me figure it out for myself. Why is that?"

"Uncle Craig, I know you. I know that you would have killed her. I lost my mother and my father. I gained a sister. I didn't want to lose another family member. Had it been me, I would have just killed you. That simple. If you were going to kill her, you would have done it as soon as you found out she was behind it. How long do you plan on torturing her?"

"Your sister will torture herself. Believe that. I'm done."

"How do you know that she's not going to try to retaliate?"

"I don't. I've had to watch my back from bigger threats than your half-sister."

"You know life is funny. Uncle Craig, did you know that you are going to be a grandfather by the woman that you hate so much. The woman that killed Cynthia is having a baby by your son. I saw the results. She's pregnant."

"She can't be. G didn't say anything. He'd tell me." It looks like I see fear in his eyes.

"He couldn't tell you something that he doesn't know. He left town before she got a chance to tell him. Now, she's going crazy over if he's ok. She worried if something happened to him. She's confused. She's hurt. She's scared. She's a mess."

"Good."

"Good? Uncle Craig, she's carrying your grandchild."

"Listen Karma, I got shit to do. This conversation is over. Thanks for the visit."

He opens his door so that I could see my way out. I know that piece of information that I gave changed the game. It may have saved Eve's life. He said that he was done, but who knows if he was telling the truth. He may not have been satisfied until she was dead and gone.

I get back in my car and I call Tori. She texted me while I was talking to Uncle Craig.

"Hello"

"Hey Tori. What's up?"

"I texted you because you were right about the tattoo needles. That's not all she did. She spray painted the words 'WATCH OUT FOR CLINGY BITCHES' on my door to the front entrance. She also took, what looks like gallons of glitter, and poured it all over my shop. My place is a fucking mess. I should beat her ass again for this."

"That's funny as hell!"

"I'm glad you're getting a kick out of this. This bitch is messing with my money. I don't live a privileged life like you Karma. My mother didn't die and leave me all of her money."

"Look. I'm sorry, but watch yourself. What my mother left me has nothing to do with you or your business." I say with an attitude.

"So, what should I do? Am I supposed to let her vandalize my shop and do nothing?"

"Did you forget that you vandalized her body by tattooing her without her permission? Yes. You should let this one slide. If she comes back to do more, then you and I will have a different conversation."

"Alright." She hangs up the phone abruptly.

My name is Karma. I am a firm believer in what goes around comes back around. If she thought that she was going to get away with what she did without anything coming back to her, she's dumb. Things always come back to you in one form or another. It may not be from the person that you did the harm to. It may come back and be delivered by somebody else. But karma is a motherfucker.

On a whim, I book a flight back to Charlotte. Eve is going to need me once I tell her this information. I can't tell her over the phone. That would be irresponsible of me.

"Hey Gina, it's Karma. I'm on the next flight to Charlotte. I want to surprise Eve. So, don't tell her that I coming. I'll see y'all tonight." I say leaving a message on Gina's voice mail.

Craig:

Karma really caught me off guard with that Eve update. She's having a baby. She's having *G's* baby. That means that it will be my grandchild. I don't know how I feel about this. On one hand, I'm excited to be a grandfather. On the second hand, the mother of my grandchild is the woman that murdered Cynthia. She took love out of my life and now has the power to give it back. I've always believed in not punishing kids for adult mistakes. That belief is why Eve is alive today. She would have been killed along with her family if I believed anything different.

I need to do a check up on Eve. I need to confirm this pregnancy. If she really is pregnant with my grandchild, I'll need to make sure that she is taking care of herself. Maybe, I can petition for custody of her baby after the baby is born. That'll really fuck with her. Listen to me talking like I'm going to be taking care of a baby. This child is G's. It's time to talk.

"Yo G!' I have to yell because he has the music up.

"What's up Craig?"

"I sent you out there to fuck with shorty's head and instead you knock her up. That wasn't part of the assignment."

"I knocked her up? I never knock women up. Who told you that she was pregnant?"

"Karma told me. You know that girl is thorough. She wouldn't have come to me with anything other than concrete information."

"How do we play this out? A baby changes everything"

"A baby doesn't change anything."

"What do you mean? It means everything. I won't have my seed out there not knowing me. I can't make believe that I never met Eve or that she's not pregnant. I did what I did for you. I see how messed up you've been since Cynthia got shot. I wanted to give you back whatever peace I could provide. My love and loyalty to my family is evident. You are telling me that I am having a baby. I have an opportunity to build a family of my own. How could you not see how this changes things? I gotta get back to Charlotte."

BAM! G stumbles, but doesn't fall to the ground.

"We laying hands on each other now?" G screams.

"That was my first and last attempt at knocking some sense into you. Loyalty ain't seasonal."

G starts to walk out. He is shaking his head. He has enough sense not to strike back.

"Being a dad shouldn't be seasonal either." He slams the door as he leaves.

Believe in Karma

Joan:

One minute life is beating you down and you have no idea how you're going to gather the strength to get back up. The next minute life is offering possibilities of happiness. Life is giving you hope. Life is giving you love. Mom told me not to worry about finding someone to love me. She would say that love would find me when I'm least expecting it. *"The packaging may be different from what you expected, but don't let it fool you; it will be your gift. You just have to be willing to receive it and open it."*

My Mom was so right. I'm not surprised. She always had some good wisdom to share. She did get one thing wrong; this gift has the same packaging as me. Ha! Thanks to David, us having the same packaging will be no more. He is paying for me to have my surgery. He has been such a blessing to me. I truly believe he was sent from God. He's been so understanding and patient with me.

We decided to practice celibacy. We both decided that it would be healthier for our relationship. I felt guilty a few times and offered to let him hit it from the back. He told me no and that he is going to wait for me to get my new coochie. I reminded him that it is not like I can walk into the hospital and walk out with a coochie; it's a process. He said that he's willing to wait. In the meantime, he will handle his business in private.

There's no pressure in this relationship. It is easy. This is what relationships are supposed to be like. If a relationship stresses you out more than it provides peace; let it go. If you walk into the same room as your partner and your spirit changes; let it go. If all of the drama in your life stems from their drama; let it go. The person that you are supposed to be with is waiting on you

191

to figure out, that the one you are with is not for you. Stop blocking your blessings. Often, we can't get to what God wants for us because we won't let go of what we know; even when we know it is bad for us. We just have to let go and trust that God will work it out. My life is a perfect example of God working things out.

This relationship is helping me to become less insecure. I'm becoming more open. I smile more. I laugh more. I am in love with this man. I even love David in our arguments. We've had an argument and I thought for sure he would change my pronoun; but he didn't. He didn't refer to me as being a man. Typically, in arguments, there are no rules to be followed. I'm used to people going for the gut when arguing; not David. At no point, did he refer to me as a man out of anger. That impressed me. He is so respectful. And he is not ashamed to show affection in public. When he takes me out, he holds me on his arm with pride. He introduces me to his friends and co-workers as his future wife. I blush with so much joy when he does that. Life is good.

It gets better. I met an older woman that wants to start a business as a salon owner, but doesn't want to be hands on. It's a woman that just wants to handle the books. She doesn't do hair, but thought that it could be a lucrative business. I talked her into letting me manage it and do hair. I'll be the face of the salon and she'll be behind the scenes collecting money from all the business I'd generate. She offered me 20% ownership of the business and said that having a stake in the business would make it harder for me to leave. She also said that once I started generating the amount of business that I promised, I could save up and buy into the business at a greater percentage. If I get enough money, we could become equal partners. I signed on the dotted line. I'm on my way to building my brand. Maybe I'll make enough money to buy her out one day. I've always been a big thinker.

I have no complaints. My work life is good. My relationship is great. I've even reconnected with Karma. She's been going through a lot lately with her family. I've tried to be there for her like she was there for me when I was down and out. Although I was a stranger, she still showed compassion and kindness. As her friend, I owe her my support. She's really had a tough year. I told her that she needs to think about practicing celibacy. Karma needs to get a hold on her life. She uses sex as a way to cope with the things that are absent in her life. Despite the suggestion, she's not willing to stop having sex; but, she agreed to keep it to a select few. She is still dealing with her sister's ex-boyfriend, Richard. I have a bad feeling about that. Eve still doesn't know that they've been seeing each other. God forbid the day that she finds out. I'll continue to pray for Karma.

Claudia:

Life is changing. I'm becoming more dependent on Rochelle. She's always video-taping me. She tells me that it will be a good way for me to remember without remembering. I let her do it. I've never been one to shy away from attention. Plus, I always thought that I should have had my own reality show anyway. Better yet a movie. Could you imagine a movie about my family? It would have had to happen while Ava was still alive. She would have stolen the show!

Karma would have given me a run for my money. She would have gotten all the viewership of the freaks. All she does is have sex. I think she has sex more than she eats. That child has problems. She doesn't care who she is doing either. She'll sleep with a man, a woman or both at the same time if they are down. What am I saying? Karma wouldn't give me a run for my money. She'd have me beat! Hoes get all of the viewership.

Rochelle has been a life saver. I forget all types of shit these days. When she's not at the house, she calls to check in on me all of the damn time. Even though she tries to play it off as if she is calling to see if I need something while she's out. Sometimes she'll talk to me her entire ride home from wherever she is coming from. She says that she needs to make sure I'm not at home alone cutting up her clothes because I forgot that we made up. She's a silly bitch. I love her to death.

I started fucking Alvin again. It happened that night that I tried to introduce Karma to the real members of her dysfunctional family. Alvin came back to my house in Milton to have a drink and talk about old times. Next thing you know, I'm giving it up. He made me write down on a piece of paper that I agreed to have sex with him, just in case I forgot that I consented. I wanted some dick, so I wrote it down. Who would have imagined, he and I would be doing each other fifty years later?

I would have been the first one to say something like that could never happen. I lived most of my life hating him and taking it out on my daughter. Never say never, because life will shake shit up in your life and "never" becomes now. Karma still won't talk to me. It's been a few months. She only speaks to me on a need to basis. Even when we speak, she doesn't call. It is always through text. I can't tell you the last time that I heard her voice. It makes me sad, but I don't say anything. I figure it is payback from the way that I treated Ava growing up. Ava named her daughter right. Karma is a bitch.

Craig came over to the house. Something was bothering him. I could tell, but he wouldn't open up about it. We sat for a while and talked about Ava. It is still hard for me to believe that she's gone. We had a lot to work on. I thought that we had more time than that. I kept saying that I was going to have a real heart-to-heart with her. At that point, I was going to tell her about her lineage. I just thought I had more time.

Unless someone is terminally ill, you never expect someone to be here today and be gone tomorrow. The truth is, it can happen to any of us. I will say that there's something extra harsh about not leaving this earth before your child does. It's a different type of pain, a different type of suffering. Thinking about it makes me sick to my stomach. I know that I didn't deliver Ava, but she's been mine since she's been in the world. I could have done a better job showing her love.

I had many opportunities to tell her that I am sorry and ashamed for how I treated her. I didn't take them. I kept putting it off. I kept putting it off until I no longer had the opportunity. That saying "there's no time like the present" is the truth. You don't know if you are going to be here tomorrow. If there is something that you've been meaning to say or do. Don't put it off. You'll be sorry if you do. I will regret the missed opportunity for the rest of my life.

"Ava, if you can hear me; I'm sorry."

BJ:

Karma and Victoria can have each other. I'm so over them. I will admit. I was acting a little crazy after they did me the way that they did. I was acting crazy because I felt crazy. My old love and who I thought was my new love were doing each other. How do things like that happen? Do they only happen to me? It sure feels like it.

After I vandalized Karma's car and Victoria's shop, I had to get myself in check. The fact that I behaved that way, told a bigger story. That showed that they still had control over me on some sick level because I lost my self-control. I allowed someone else to drive me to do things that I got enough sense to know not to do. I was even thinking about contacting Eve to ask her if she knew her sister slept with her ex-boyfriend Richard after Ava's funeral. I knew I needed help.

I went to on my health insurance website and found a therapist that was in network with my plan. I called her up and took her first open appointment. I needed to get my life back. Since I've been dealing with Karma, I've been going downhill fast. I'm sure I could have used a therapist before now. It took me running into Karma to admit that I needed help and seek it. This isn't my first unhealthy relationship. If you ask my Aunt Clara, she'd tell you that all of my relationships have been unhealthy. She believes my lifestyle is sick. She's been wanting me to see a therapist for years, but for different reasons. She wanted me to stop being a dyke.

Now, I'm seeing a therapist and she's wonderful. She gets me. I don't go a week without seeing her. We are going to address my need to be in a relationship next week. I think I know where this is going. I can tell by the way that she smiles at me. I notice the way that she says my name. She says it so sweetly. It's like she sings it each time she calls my name. I can't lie. I've daydreamed about what it would be like to be with her.

She's so lovely. I wonder if she day dreams about me. On our next visit, I will ask her. I will ask her if she thinks about how soft my lips would feel against hers. I will ask her if she's ever touched herself while thinking about me. I know I have. I think about her throughout the week. I wonder what she's doing. I wonder who she is with.

I couldn't stand the wait. I called her office today to find out if I could get an extra session in. She had a cancellation. It must be fate. When I get into her office, I will take her into my arms and tell her that I know we are supposed to be together. I will tell her how special she is to me. I will then tell her that I love her.

Karma:

I dreamt about my mother last night. She was trying to tell me something. Every time she tried to say what she had to say, she got interrupted. She never told me. I woke up feeling like what she had to say was very important. I tried to go back to sleep, just so I could dream about her again. I wanted to give her a chance to tell me but I couldn't get back to sleep.

I am up now. I feel a little off. Something just doesn't feel right. I'm hoping this isn't a precursor to a bad day. I've had enough of those. I had a cold for the last two months. For some reason, I can't get rid of it. I figure my immune system must be on overload. I've been stressed dealing with my sister's issues; on top of the issues I'm avoiding in Massachusetts. I went to a walk-in clinic and had them run some tests on me.

Eve hasn't been doing well. I've been back and forth to Charlotte for the past three months trying to make sure she is ok. She had to take a leave of absence from work. She just couldn't get it together. The night that I arrived in Charlotte, after finding out about G, Eve had a break down. She miscarried on her way back from G's last known address. I felt so bad for her.

She was so excited about having this baby. She had even talked to me about having a single mom mind-set. She wasn't going to put out a search party for Greg. She wasn't going to look for any type of support. If he could leave her the way that he did, he didn't deserve to be in their lives. I really thought she was getting stronger. I was proud of her. Then she miscarried and that tipped her over the edge.

Gina didn't know how to handle her in this state. So, she asked if Eve should go to a psychiatric hospital. I asked Gina if she got sent to a psych hospital every time she acted crazy. From what I heard, Gina was on and off drugs during Eve's entire life. Eve took care of her and the rest of the house the best way that she could. It's now Gina's turn. She admitted that she was scared, but is willing to give Eve the best that she has.

Gina got a job. She couldn't be there with Eve twenty-four seven. The first month, I stayed with Eve. When Gina got off from work, it was her turn to take over the shift. I'd then spend most nights with Richard. Gina and Eve thought that I was staying at a hotel. I let them believe it. If there was ever a time to come clean about what's been going on with Richard and I this was not the time.

I didn't really have any time to find any new bedroom interests while in Charlotte. My time was spent with Eve and then with Richard. Being in Charlotte and only sleeping with Richard, showed me that I could be monogamous. For a while, I didn't believe that I could be satisfied by one person. Richard keeps me satisfied. The only problem with that is he and I could never be. We can continue to sneak around, but I couldn't be in a relationship with him and still have my sister's love. She'd hate me. I love my sister more than I love being with Richard.

She's my blood. It feels good to be there for someone and to have someone there for you. I will say that Joan really stepped up. She's been a great listener. I've dropped some heavy shit on her and she's been a superstar when it comes to being a friend. Her life is finally taking a turn for the better. She found a man that doesn't care that she has a dick. I didn't care that she had a dick either, but she wouldn't give me any play. Ha! Ha! Let me stop. Anyway, Joan's been a good friend and Eve's been a good sister.

Uncle Craig is acting like a piece of shit. I told him that Eve miscarried. He showed no compassion. He said that the baby knew that it's mother wasn't worth a damn and aborted itself. He said he owes the baby because it saved him the trouble of aborting the baby himself. I knew Uncle Craig could be cruel, but it never had an effect on me because his cruelty never extended to my family. He and I haven't spoken since that conversation.

Being in Charlotte has been good for me. Although, I came out here due to unfortunate circumstances; it's good to be away from the drama I left in Boston. I let things fizzle down with Tori. She is too much of a hot head. She reminds me of girls that live in a group home. The kind that have a chip on their shoulder. They feel that since they got dealt a bad hand in life, they have the right to overreact about minor shit. They take their pain out on whoever crosses their path.

I believe in "an eye for an eye", but Tori has a different philosophy. She is from the same school of thought as Uncle Craig. They believe that if someone sticks out their foot and trips you, the offender should get their foot cut off. That way they can't trip anyone again. Their thinking is a little extreme, even for me.

I never heard from BJ after she threw a brick through my car window shield. She must have found someone else to latch on to. I swear that girl must have been neglected her entire childhood. She is so damn needy. I asked Tori if she heard from her again. She said that she hadn't but if she does see her again, that she's busting her ass again. BJ cost her a lot of money with the shop. She had to shut it down for two days to get things back in order. She takes it personal when somebody messes with her money. I question if she remembers what *she* did to BJ. She's lucky that's all BJ did.

I have a follow up appointment to go over the test results later today. I hope they find out what is going on with me. I need to start feeling like myself again. Last night, Richard wore me out. We only went two rounds and I was beat. I couldn't hang. He and I both know that two rounds are like warm up rounds. For me to be spent after two rounds worries me. Maybe, I need to start taking vitamins. I haven't been going to the gym as frequently as I used to. I've just been busy. I can't imagine what's going on with me.

I've been doing a lot of thinking. I'm going to go home next month. I'm going to give Rochelle, Alvin and my grandmother a chance to win me over. I'm sure that they all had their reasons. The least that I can do is hear them out. There's no time like the present. I call my grandmother's cell phone to let her know that I'll be home next month. I'll be ready to talk.

"Hello" Rochelle answers the phone. She sounds frantic.

"Hi Rochelle. It's Karma. I'm looking for my grandmother. How come you are answering her phone."

"Oh, my God Karma! Come home! You have to come home now!"

"What's going on? Why are you screaming? Where's my grandmother?"

"She left her phone in my car the last time she was in it. Karma come home. I'm standing outside of what's left of the house."

"What do you mean what's left of the house?" I ask afraid to hear the answer.

"The fireman said that the source of the fire came from the kitchen stove. She left the gas on and went to sleep. She must have forgotten that she put something on the stove."

"So, where is she? Did she get burned? Is she on her way to the hospital?"

"They couldn't get her out! She was trapped in her room. The only way that she could get out is through the window. I watched as the fireman got on a ladder to get her out through her window. She wouldn't go with him. He yelled at her to open the window. She wouldn't open it. He couldn't wait. He told her to stand back so he could break the glass."

"Then what happened."

"The fireman said that when he got inside the window, your grandmother said that her daughter Ava was calling her. She opened the bedroom door and was immediately engulfed with flames. The fireman had to escape back out of the window. He got burned, but he's alive. Your grandmother went on to be with your momma Karma. I'm so, so sorry."

"Noooooooooooo! I was coming home so that we could fix this family. I was calling to tell her that we could all sit down and talk! She can't be gone! She can't leave me too!

Is this some fucking sick joke! God wasn't happy with taking my mother and my father. He had to take my grandmother too! What could I have possibly done to deserve this? He took everyone that loves me and left me with who? He left me with my maniac Uncle Craig and my mentally ill half-sister. Good looking out God! You really know how to treat a girl! Whose sins am I paying for? I'm too young to deserve all of this heartache. There's nothing else that can happen to me that'll be worse than losing your entire family in a span of a year."

Rochelle says nothing. She just listens in silence. The only way I can tell that she's on the phone is because the timer on the phone is still going. Then she speaks.

"I'll never be able to take the place of anyone that you've lost, but I want you to know that I am going to be here for you. You are my kin. Family is supposed to be there for one another. You may not like that we are family, but you can't pick your family. Come home Karma."

"I'm on my way Grandmom."

Craig:

G connected with Karma after he stormed out of here the night that I clocked him. He wanted to go to Charlotte with her, but she talked him out of it. She told him that it was too soon. He needed to let her assess how her sister was doing in person. Once she did, she'd let him know if he should come down.

When Karma called, and told me that Eve miscarried I was glad. I couldn't wait to tell G. Things had been different between us since he found out he was going to be a daddy. I wanted things to get back to normal. I wanted my son back. He even told me to stop calling him G. His name is Greg. I thought this fool had lost his mind. Where does he get off telling me not to call him what I've called him since he's been born? I have no problem with the name Greg. What I have a problem with is him trying to check me. So, I still call him G to fuck with him. Any inch of power that he thinks he can get, he's going to try to get it. Even something as simple as telling me to refer to him as Greg; I'm not going to give him the satisfaction.

Greg, formerly known as G, came by the house when I told him I had some information about Eve and the baby.

"I talked to Karma."

"You did? What did she say? Is it cool for me to go back down to Charlotte?"

"No, she said that your baby mama is no longer your baby mama."

"Craig, stop beating around the bush, what did she say?"

"I ain't never been a man to beat around the bush. I was trying to spare my sensitive son Greg's feelings. Karma said that Eve lost the baby. She miscarried. Now, she's acting crazy so it's not a good idea for you to come down there. Karma is going to stay with her until she gets back on her feet."

The look in my son's eyes almost made me sad for him, but then I thought about who it is that lost the baby. The woman that lost the baby is the same woman that killed my lady and any hope of us having a child together. Fuck that bitch. I'm glad she is suffering. She deserves it. Greg found out that Karma is coming back to Boston to attend Claudia's funeral. He plans on going back with Karma when she leaves to Charlotte. He feels like he owes Eve an apology. I told him that if he goes to Charlotte to work things out with Eve, that he will be forgotten. I will conduct my life as if I never knew him. You can't commit treason and still want to be family. He left. He chose Eve over me.

Eve:

Karma is usually here every day. Today she's not. I asked Gina before she left for work, where she is. She told me that Karma lost her grandmother Claudia. There was a fire and Claudia wouldn't leave the house. The odd thing about today is that I'm feeling better. I got two calls today. One call was from Greg. I almost didn't recognize his voice. He was crying. He said that he was sorry and needed to come see me. I need closure. I told him to come whenever he is ready. I'm ready to hear what could have possibly made him do such a thing to me.

The second call that I get is from Richard. He said that he wanted to apologize for not fighting for our relationship. He was getting scared. Things were getting very serious for us and he wasn't sure he was ready for where things were headed with us. He said that by me accepting the job in Boston it gave him an easy out. He's sorry for making it seem like it was my fault. He also said that he's not sure if Karma told me, but they've been sleeping with each other for a year now. The only reason why he is telling me this is because he isn't sure when he contracted it, but he has HIV. He asked that I pass on that information to Karma. And just like that he hung up.

When I was tested for pregnancy, I had an HIV test. It was negative. I'm not worried about Richard's status, but it sounds like Karma should be. This is a lot of information to take in. I find out that my sister has been sleeping with my ex-man behind my back for a year. I also find out that she could be HIV positive. I don't know how to feel. I'm mad. I'm sad. I'm worried. For some reason, I feel like I can handle it. I feel stronger today. A few days ago, this may have pushed me over the edge.

Ah ha! Now I know why I woke up at peace. I dreamt about her. My biological mother, Charlene, visited me in my dream. I usually only remember my bad dreams. This dream I remember.

"Your name is Evelyn. I named you after a classy woman. She was one of my best friends. She's up here with me. Ava's up here too. We are all finally back together. I heard that Ava's mother will be up here soon. Make sure you tell Karma to slow down. She's moving too fast. I'm glad that she's taking care of you. She has a good heart. She's just like her mother. Ava always looked out for me when we were young. You two make sure you're there for one another. Life will be challenging, but you'll get through it. Never give up Evelyn. It's ok to fall, but make sure you get back up. Allow yourself to be loved. Be kind. Have compassion. Tell the truth and most importantly strengthen your relationship with God. Everything else will fall into place.'

"Mom…"

"Yes Evelyn."

"I love you."

"I loved you before I knew you Evelyn."

Then I woke up.

Rochelle:

Today would have been my daughter Ava's birthday. When she was young, I used to always celebrate her birthday with her. Claudia always made sure that I was there to cut the cake and sing happy birthday. That tradition stopped after the hair cutting incident.

That day, Claudia told me to come by because "our" daughter was mouthing off. Claudia was my ride or die. If she needed me, I was there. Things got a little out of hand. I ended up helping her hold Ava down and chop off her hair to teach her a lesson. Ava has hated me ever since. She tried to retaliate and stab me with the same scissors we cut her hair off with. She stopped dealing with me all together after that. I thought that she'd come around and forgive me, but she never did. Ava sure could hold a grudge.

It wasn't easy watching the child that I gave birth to be raised by Claudia. We definitely had different parenting styles. I had no right to say anything about it. I signed Ava over to be raised by Claudia. Even if I didn't agree with some of the ways she dealt with Ava, it wasn't my place to interfere.

Ava and Claudia didn't have a good relationship. Claudia took a lot of her pain from being rejected by Alvin out on Ava. Looking back, we really should have told Ava sooner about